CHASE JONES IS MY FAKE BOYFRIEND

RUMORS AND LIES AT EVERMORE HIGH #1

EMILY LOWRY

Cover Photography by
LOGAN WEAVER VIA UNSPLASH
Cover Design by
CANVA

 ELEVENTH AVENUE
PUBLISHING

A THANK YOU FROM EMILY

I wanted to take a moment to say thank you to my readers —
without you, none of this would be possible.

I truly appreciate every single review, Instagram post and
blog shout-out that you have given me. Every email, message
and kind word from you has brightened my day, every time.
You are the true MVPs!

To my ARC team, thank you for your endless encourage-
ment and incredibly helpful feedback. I value each and every
one of you.

Now, to write my next love story. Stay tuned!

Lots of love always,

XO, Emily

ABBY

*I*f I had to sum up high school in one word, I'd pick electric.

It was the nervous energy flowing through your body as you prepared for the first day back. The spark when the cute boy smiles. The lightning bolt of a first kiss, the thunderstorm of falling in love, the rain-swept field that follows a breakup.

At least, that's how a high school romance was supposed to feel.

Not that I would know. I could only imagine what everyone else's high school experience must be like. You know, the jocks, the cheerleaders, the popular kids and homecoming queens and class clowns and student body presidents. Everyone. Well, everyone but me.

I'd held on to that energy, that electricity, all summer. But instead of going out and having all the clichéd high school experiences the rest of my grade were having before their junior year, I'd poured my entire summer into a single story for our school newspaper, The Panther Pinnacle. It was a perfect piece of investigative journalism. The kind of hard-hitting exposé my heroes — Minna Lewinson and Diane Sawyer — would be proud of.

I put the story in a binder and snapped the clips closed. The paper was perfect. It had to be perfect. I was bringing it to my journalism prof first thing this morning, as proof that I had what it took to be the investigative reporter for The Pinnacle this year. I had a perfect plan: I'd hold that position for my junior year, take over as lead editor in my senior year, then after that? NYU. Just like my mom.

My chosen outfit for my first day back at school was already hanging on the door, freshly washed and neatly ironed. I had picked it out weeks ago. I wanted something that would convey that I was professional, yet approachable. Intellectual, yet worldly. Not that my closet had offered too much to convey all that, and Dad had been too stingy to lend me fifty bucks to buy something new. All in all, I was happy with the plaid, pleated skirt, button-down shirt and loafers I picked out for today's occasion. I added a tight ponytail and my reading glasses, and voila! — I nailed it. Perfect female journalist with prime lead editor potential.

I was ready for the first day of my junior year.

EVERMORE HIGH WAS a sprawling campus of brick buildings, athletic fields, flower gardens, fountains, and stunning views of the Rocky Mountains. It was a hive of activity, home to just over two thousand students.

It was a fairy tale place — but by fairy tale I'm talking Brothers Grimm, not Disney. Cliques reigned over their subjects, rewarding and punishing them with a sense of poetic justice. Rumors spread like a summer fire over a cornfield, and truth? Truth was relative.

Honestly, I expected better from the kids of our large

Denver suburb. Colorado was meant to be a progressive place... but Evermore was like every bad high school movie: finding your clique was your lifeline for a social life.

Nobody at school even read the Pinnacle, the paper I loved so much and worked so hard on. They didn't need to. Anything you wanted to know could be found on the school's notorious — and conveniently anonymous — gossip app, Click.

I had never been featured on Click, and I knew all too well I never would be. I was one of the Evermore cliqueless — by choice, as I reminded my dad every time he asked why I didn't go out with friends more. I was happy being invisible, coasting through the hallways unnoticed, gathering the grades and achievements I needed to guarantee I got into NYU. I didn't want, need, or desire to be at the center of a school scandal. I would leave that to the popular kids, thank you very much.

I hurried through the throngs of students. The seniors laughed loudly to draw attention, the guys fist bumping each other while the girls smoothed their hair, hoping someone would notice the new styles they got over the summer. A whole new year of possibilities lay ahead. The freshmen congregated in tight packs, their voices hoarse whispers.

And me?

I continued to be invisible, the way a good journalist should be. Maybe that's why I was so obsessed with journalism — I didn't want to be part of the rumors, but I wanted to know about them. I treated my high school like I was reading it in a book instead of living it.

The school paper had its own office on the second floor of Building A, which was the Fine Arts Building. The door had textured glass, and when I opened it, the smell of coffee overpowered every other sense. We always had two coffee pots going — either brewing or burning, depending on whether the last one out had remembered to shut them off.

"Abigail Murrow! Welcome back." The warm, friendly voice had a thin Nigerian accent and belonged to my favorite teacher, Mr. Adebayo. He was in his fifties and wore a crisp, white dress shirt. As the year went on, that shirt would accumulate coffee stains. By June, the shirt would be more brown than white.

A senior stood next to Mr. Adebayo, smiling at me.

My heart skipped a beat.

It wasn't just any senior.

Nicholas Applebee. His hair was casually combed to the side, and he wore thin glasses which framed his face perfectly. He had the charming smile of a morning newscaster. And he was this year's lead editor of The Pinnacle.

I smiled back, keeping my lips closed so the butterflies didn't escape from my stomach. I had worked with Nicholas on the Pinnacle since freshman year, and I still couldn't get it together when he was around me. He was the weak spot in my perfect plan of keeping all of my thoughts and efforts focused on NYU.

He poured a cup of coffee and passed me the mug. "Abs! Just the person I was looking for."

My heart lurched again. I suspected it would get quite the workout with the time I'd be spending with Nicholas.

"Great! I was looking for me too!" I stuttered. Uh, no, that wasn't right. "You. I was looking for you." I finished, my cheeks flaring.

I looked at him to see if he had noticed my stutter and blush, but he wasn't looking at me, he was focused on the binder in my hand. "What's that, Abby? A story? You can't possibly have a story ready. We haven't even gone over this semester's assignments."

I laughed, too loud and too long. I wasn't sure if he was

making a joke or not. Call my laughter a nervous reflex. I passed him the binder. "I did some digging over the summer on the nastiness that goes on behind school board elections. Hard-hitting stuff."

He opened the binder and read. His expression faltered. "I see."

A lump formed in my throat. I thought he'd be excited that I'd got an early start. Why wasn't he smiling? I'd spent all summer on that piece.

Nicholas glanced at Mr. Adebayo, who nodded, then back to me. "Can we talk?"

Three words no one ever wants to hear.

Nicholas led me into the editor's office and shut the door. Framed articles hung from the wall, the paper yellowed with age. There was a shelf of neatly stacked books in the back corner. Through the closed door, I heard the other members of the school paper chatting, their voices muffled.

I couldn't stand the tension.

"So, what do you think?" I blurted, my hands clammy.

He drummed his fingers over the paper. "I met with Mr. Adebayo about a week before school started. We talked about you."

What? Why? Was that good? Bad?

The suspense was killing me.

"You're a talented writer with great potential." Nicholas sighed, taking off his glasses and polishing them on his shirt.

There was a but coming.

"But your range is narrow. You want to go to NYU, right?"

He remembered! I nodded, my smile tight and forced. "Like my mom."

"They'll want a portfolio, Abby."

"I have one," I insisted, looking at him strangely. What was coming?

"And what's in it?"

I rattled off a list of investigate reports I'd finished. I had published almost all of them in the Panther Pinnacle over the last couple of years. Why was Nicholas asking? He was the person who reviewed ninety percent of my work. That's why his opinion mattered so much.

"All investigative pieces," he said.

"That's what I want to do." The chair I was sitting in suddenly felt very uncomfortable. "If you want to be an investigative journalist, you investigate. Practice makes perfect."

"We have some concerns." Nicholas said flatly.

I felt like I was being deflated.

"Is my writing not good enough?" That couldn't be it. I was known around school — by those who knew me, at least — as the girl who writes. It was practically my entire identity.

To my surprise, Nicholas laughed. "You're the best writer at the Pinnacle, Abby. Myself included. It's your range that's concerning. You've got the talent to get into NYU, but when they ask for a portfolio, Mr. Adebayo says they'll want to see a range of different types of journalism. Which is why we've pulled you off investigative journalism for the semester."

My brain short-circuited. I was — in their words — the best writer they had. I loved investigative journalism. And they were pulling me off of it? All of my hopes and dreams for my junior year felt like they were running through my hands, and I could not catch them.

I almost didn't dare ask the next question that came to my mind. "What are you moving me to?"

"The social feature."

"THE SOCIAL FEATURE?" I screeched.

Imagine a wrecking ball crashing through a china shop and you'll know how I felt. My mouth was suddenly dry. The social feature was — in my opinion — the lamest, fluffiest part of the school paper. It was basically a glorified gossip column, for goodness sake! Nothing I cared about. And nothing like the hard-hitting investigative journalism that would get me into NYU.

Nicholas clasped his hands together, excited. "I pitched it to Mr. Adebayo this morning. I want a full feature on the social life of a student at Evermore. What's it like to go to parties? Where do people go on dates? How does one navigate interpersonal relationships? What about dealing with all the rumors and lies that come with being part of the social fabric of our high school? It will be an amazing feature, and we hope we will significantly increase our readership with it!"

I sighed. He was right about nobody reading the paper at school. But if people wanted gossip, they wouldn't come to the paper, they'd open Click and check who was on blast. Plus, I was hardly the best person to write a gossip column.

"Shouldn't Payton do that?" Payton was one of the other juniors working at the paper. Pretty, relatively popular, and the daughter of the head football coach, Payton Clarence was much more intertwined with the Evermore 'social fabric' than I'd ever be.

"She wanted to do sports again this year," Nicholas said. Of course she did, I thought flatly. If there was ever a way to get close to the football players, it was as our sports reporter. It's the sort of perk that makes people like Payton work at the paper. I couldn't deny how bitter my thoughts were.

Nicholas looked at me, his eyes bright with excitement. "And also, I think you'll write a marvelous story. I believe in you. Do well here, and you'll be the senior editor next year." He grinned. "So, what do you say? Is my all-star reporter ready to dive in?"

Panic and butterflies battled in my chest as my thoughts

also fought for space in my mind: He came up with the idea and assigned it to me because he thought it would be better for my future. But I had never even been to a high school party. He believed in me. Did anyone else? He thought I was "his" all-star.

"How could I say no?" I said weakly.

"Great!" Nicholas looked at me approvingly, his hazel eyes warm.

I tried to look enthusiastic, but inside, my brain was screaming at me.

There was one teeny tiny little problem: how was I supposed to write the social feature when I didn't have a social life?

CHASE

*W*alking through the Fine Arts Building of the Evermore campus, I was as out of place as a bull in a museum. Colorful abstract paintings hung from the walls, tiny bronze plaques beneath each one naming the artist and the painting.

Tides of Animal.

Broken Drop Drip.

The Ease of Our Sorrows and the Joy in Our Pains.

I can't say I understood any of them. Art had never really been my thing.

I passed an open door along the hallways. Inside, the drama club had set up black stools in a semi-circle. They were wearing masks, acting out some weird play, and as I passed by, they all craned their necks towards me. It was like something out of a horror movie. I shuddered, almost laughing at myself. The starting quarterback, fearless when going against a three-hundred-pound sasquatch that wanted to tackle me, nervous around dainty drama club geeks wearing masks. If anyone on the team found out I also couldn't sit through a horror movie, I'd never hear the end.

I focused on my mission, feeling excited. Savannah, the girl I was sort-of dating, spent almost all of her time in the Fine Arts building. We'd only been seeing each other for the last three weeks, a perfect end to the summer holidays, but somehow, we were already splashed all over Click. Even during summer vacation, Evermore students had their way of keeping the rumor mill running. Gossip was like oxygen at Evermore, everyone breathed it in.

Savannah was a ballet dancer, and a good one at that. Last week, I picked her up from her ballet studio downtown. I was there early enough to watch the end of practice. Watching her dance was spellbinding. Her slim, pale body stretched gracefully into impossible positions. Her dedication and focus reminded me of my own game on the football field, striving for nothing short of perfection in every move I made.

It helped that Savannah was smoking hot, with baby blue eyes and long red hair, coupled with a svelte dancer's body. I had to admit, for the first time in what seemed like forever, I was totally taken with a girl.

I hadn't seen her at all yet this morning during our first day back at Evermore. It was my junior year, her senior one, so we shared no classes. However, during morning break, she'd sent me a text telling me to come find her. She wanted to talk to me about our next date.

I had already planned it out. She was a huge animal lover, so I'd spent my very meager pay check on tickets to the zoo. But not just any tickets — the zoo's equivalent of a backstage pass. We'd get to meet the zookeepers and see how things worked behind the scenes. We'd also get to feed and interact with the less dangerous animals. She would love it.

Savannah was sweet and quiet — not my usual type. But after breaking up with Madison Albright last year and finding myself subsequently hacked apart on her hugely popular Click page, my attraction to the bouncy, peppy cheerleader type — which honestly, was so boringly predictable when you thought about it — went out the window.

As I navigated the halls, I heard a choir warming up and the distant sound of the concert band tuning their instruments. I took off my letterman jacket, rolled it, and carried it under my arm like a football. It was warm out anyway, and always warmer still in the Fine Arts building than any of the other buildings on campus. Or maybe I was just overheating because I was nervous. Why was I nervous?

The dance studio was at the back of the building. Savannah stood outside, already finished with practice, and dressed in black tights and a wrap sweater. She didn't smile when I approached. That was okay, she probably had a lot on her mind with it being the first day of school.

"How's your first day back going?" I asked. I wished I thought of something cooler to say. Something smooth.

"Okay," she said. "Come in."

Savannah led me into the dance studio. It was painted white and there was a ballet bar at one end. Bay windows faced the mountains and let in plenty of natural light. I was struck by how high the ceiling was. You could toss a decent pass in here.

"I've never been in here before," I said. "It's nice."

"Not much of a dancer?" Savannah laughed gently.

"Coach actually says I should take it. Says it'll keep my feet quick, help me move around the pocket."

"Are you going to?" Savannah bit her bottom lip.

"No."

"That's good." She visibly relaxed.

Good?

Savannah nervously pulled her hair back in a ponytail. "I had a lot of fun with you these past weeks, Chase."

She still wasn't smiling. She wasn't making eye contact either. My stomach dropped. I knew where this conversation was heading. I'd been on the receiving end of it at the start of summer, too. I had never been broken up with in my life and then - BAM - three times in a row.

"But?" I kept my voice calm and even, but I felt like someone was punching me in the gut.

"It's not working for me." Savannah leveled, her voice flat.

What had happened? I'd seen Savannah two days ago, on Saturday, and she had been looking at me adoringly the whole time. I'd turned on the charm, wanting to impress her, and I thought it had worked.

Today, I was face to face with a totally different person. In fact, it was three weeks to the day Savannah and I started seeing each other. As much as I wanted to deny it — especially in that moment — I'd really liked her, too. More than anyone since Madison. Madi and I had dated for almost a year before I eventually broke up with her a few months ago. I had liked - maybe even loved - her, especially at first. She was my first serious girlfriend, and I guess that would always mean something. But, after seeing her true colors coming out in a flurry of horrible mean-girl comments and behaviors, and having to question more than once if she liked me for me or my quarterback status, I had called it quits. Sadly.

Mean or not, Madi was unquestionably the hottest girl at school, and I was only human.

"Can you tell me why?" I asked, focusing my thoughts back on Savannah, standing in front of me. You couldn't improve if you didn't know what the problem was. I braced myself.

"Sorry," Savannah said. She gave me a quick hug. I felt the warmth of her hands on my shoulders. Her hair smelled like roses. She squeezed once, almost regretfully, then dipped out of the studio, leaving me alone.

I rested against the wall, sliding to my butt like I was a cartoon character. Every high school movie I'd ever watched showed the QB getting the girl. But the movies were lies. Savannah was the third girl to break up with me in a matter of months, and man was it weird.

Not to sound arrogant, but I wasn't used to this... and this was now strike three.

First there was Phoebe, in the spring, not long after Madi and I broke up. She offered me "a shoulder to cry on" and her shoulders were tan and smooth and covered by long, blonde hair. I had accepted, needing a rebound, and actually, Phoebe and I, we got along pretty well. She was a bit of an antidote to Madison. I was warming up to her when, three weeks later, she dropped off the face of the earth. Never texted me back. I didn't bother seeking an explanation at the time, but maybe I should have. Every time I saw her in the hallways at school after that, she would look the other direction, like she hadn't seen me.

I didn't lose any sleep over it, and didn't really think too much about it.

But then, at the start of the summer, I went out with this chick, Ella, from the private school across town for a bit. Tried to see if something was there, but we didn't mesh. It felt like our conversations stumbled into each other, like we were never quite talking about the same thing. Three weeks of romantic comedies and ice cream didn't help.

Then, three weeks to the day we first showed up on Click, she blindsided me.

"Get out of my life, Chase Jones. And stay out."

I. Was. Stumped. Sure, we obviously weren't connecting on anything more than a physical level. But the hostility? Totally unwarranted.

Today, here with Savannah, I was gutted. I'd really liked her. I hadn't even been texting other girls back in the time I'd been seeing her, no matter how much my phone blew up. I must have been doing something wrong. I wished someone would tell me what.

I pulled out my phone and texted Dylan, our starting running back. If I could count on anyone to give it to me straight, it was Dylan Ramirez. He has been my best friend through elementary and middle school, before my knack for throwing a football had become apparent. He was the one who had caught on that both Phoebe and Ella had dumped me three weeks into our fledgling relationships.

Chase: She dumped me.

My phone buzzed.

Dylan: Dude. Seriously?

Chase: Just now.

Dylan: You good?

Chase: Yeah.

Dylan: She say why?

Chase: Said it wasn't working for her.

Dylan: Dude I don't even know what that means. Sorry man.

Chase: All good.

Dylan: She dump you at three weeks?

Chase: Exactly three weeks since the first Click post of us together. Same as last time.

Dylan: Dude. It's a curse. You better break the cycle next time.

Chase: Don't I know it.

I pocketed my phone. I'd forgotten about the weird three-week curse temporarily. Otherwise I might not have spent all that money on the zoo. Ugh, the zoo.

I texted Dylan again

Chase: I got a spare third period. Think I'm gonna take off for a bit. Want to join?

Dylan: Already in history my dude.

Chase: All good. Also. This weekend. Want to come to the zoo?

Dylan: I thought you'd never ask. It's a date. You should know though, I don't put out on the first date, k?

I grinned.

Chase: Fine by me, just don't ditch me three weeks from now.

3

ABBY

I was still in complete disbelief when I left the Pinnacle office. Me. Abigail Murrow. Star investigative journalist. Shoved aside, relegated to cover the ridiculous, never-ending popularity contest that was high school life at Evermore. Picking me for this assignment was like picking a fish to cross a desert. No matter how much anyone — even Nicholas Applebee — believed in the fish, it would end up shriveled and miserable.

The school paper office was located in the Fine Arts Building, so I was used to random Shakespeare quotations echoing through the halls. This year, it looked like the drama club had decided on Macbeth, but with vampires. Anything to capture that coveted teen market. I felt their pain.

I had more pressing concerns than the opening night audience, however. I was borderline invisible in the school's hierarchy, so how was I supposed to write any kind of feature on what it was like to be popular?

At the other end of the hallway, the door to the dance studio opened. I waited for a parade of ballerinas to spin across the linoleum. Instead, I was greeted by a most unusual sight:

Chase Jones, all-star quarterback for Evermore High.

Chase is something of a legend here at Evermore, and he's only a junior. Last year, in his sophomore year, Chase was named starting quarterback for the Evermore Panthers — a feat that was almost unheard of. He led the team to their first division win in a decade, before bowing out in the playoffs to the eventual state champions. If you believed the rumors, he was one of the best quarterbacks in his grade nationwide, and would likely have several full-ride scholarships waiting for him when he finished school. I'd never spoken to him, but I assumed he was exactly the same as what I assumed the other football players were like: self-centered, egotistical, and obsessed with his own reflection.

Chase Jones was one of those guys. You know the sort - perfect, floppy hair, dreamy eyes, and an All-American smile that girls go weak at the knees for. So cliché.

Everything I knew about Chase Jones I learned through Click: He got his dark, brooding looks from his ex-college football star dad and Puerto Rican model mom; he was aiming to get a full ride at a Division 1 football school - apparently Texas A&M and Ole Miss were already sniffing around; since his famed break up with Evermore's most popular girl, Madison Albright, he had been pictured with a string of girlfriends, none of them lasting long.

At the moment, none of that mattered. Right now, he was just a boy, staring at the ground, looking lost. No band of bros or adoring fans to pump him up. I had to wonder though, what in the world was our quarterback doing in the Fine Arts Building? What in the world was he doing in a DANCE STUDIO?

An idea popped into my mind, like a lightbulb had suddenly flicked on.

Maybe I didn't have to be popular to write the social feature.

Maybe I just had to talk to people who were popular.

And who better to start with than one of the most popular guys on campus?

A burst of sudden confidence came over me. I could do this! This was my way to nail the social feature!

"Chase?"

Without looking to see who was calling him, Chase took off.

Jerk.

I put my hands on my hips. "Yeah, yeah... Be as rude as you want, Jones. I'm not letting you off the hook that easy."

And then, for some reason unknown to anyone, especially myself, I ran after him. What was I doing?!

Unfortunately, he was an all-star athlete. Six foot three, with long legs to match.

I was a sort-of in-shape journalist. Five foot five, with stubby legs that made me believe one of my parents was secretly a peg-legged pirate. Even at a light jog, Chase easily outpaced me. I expected him to head to the Athletics Building, but he was angling towards the parking lot.

Good. If we were both in our cars, at least I'd have a chance at catching him.

Chase climbed in a black Jeep that was parked at the back of the lot. For the first time, I saw his face as he glanced in his rearview mirror. It was tight, pinched.

What had happened to Chase Jones on our first day back? And why wasn't it already all over Click? Suddenly, I felt like I just HAD to find out.

Chase stopped carefully at the exit, then pulled onto the road, heading east. By that time, I was already in my trusty rust bucket of a car, ready to pursue.

"It's okay, Abby. You're not a stalker," I reassured myself. "You're just a journalist."

4

CHASE

$\mathcal{I}$ didn't know where I was going, I just knew I didn't want to stay on campus. I wanted to get away and... wallow for a while. Without thinking, I jumped in my Jeep and drove towards Main Street.

The first thing you need to know about our town's Main Street is that it feels like it was pulled straight from the 1950s, complete with vintage street lamps and brick side-walks. You won't find a Starbucks or a McDonalds there — every shop on Main Street is locally owned and classified as a Heritage building. Big businesses couldn't buy them and turn them into franchises even if they wanted to.

Main Street was also not technically a street. At least, not for cars. About a decade ago, the town took the step to turn it into a pedestrian-only zone. That didn't stop cyclists from zipping through, but at least they were courteous enough to use their bells.

I parked a block away. I crossed the street without looking properly, and as a result, I almost got hit by a girl driving a car so rusted I was amazed it was still running. She mouthed "sorry" at me, her face contorted in a shocked "O" shape. I waved and headed for Main Street. First emotionally, now almost literally, I was getting run over today. Great start to the year, Chase. You'll probably get cut from the team, too.

It was relatively early in the day, but most of the shops were already open. People — seniors, mostly — mingled and dipped in and out of the colorful storefronts. A woman who would've been my grandmother's age, if she was still with us, compared two plant vases. The first was blue with an orange sunset. The second was white with circles of colorful vines.

She caught my eye and smiled. "I don't know why I buy these things. I can't seem to keep anything I put in them alive."

I laughed warmly. "If it's any consolation, my twin sister gave me a cactus for my birthday and I watered it too much so it died."

True story. Jordyn had been outraged and said I must be the only person on earth to have ever killed a cactus by trying to care about it too much. I'd rolled my eyes in response and told her to get me something useful - like a sweater - on our next birthday. We were super tight, Jordyn and I, she was one of my best friends. When she wasn't being a royal pain in my butt.

"Aren't we a pair?" The old lady eyed the vases and then eyed me. "Which one do you think goes better with a dead plant?"

"The sunset. Definitely." I responded without thinking.

"You sound sure."

"I know my dead plants." I smiled at her. Nice old lady.

She laughed. "Sunset it is."

I carried the vase to the front counter for her and made sure the clerk would help her take it to her car. Then I wandered further up the street to my favorite yogurt place, Peak Crossing Frozen Yogurt. Peak's for short.

I walked in, pleased to find I was the only person in the shop, save for the grumpy, middle-aged cashier, who looked irked by my presence.

I stood still for a second, relishing the anonymity. I felt a bit better.

Or at least I did for a second, until I heard the bell on the door jingle behind me. I turned to see the girl who had almost hit me with her car just standing there, gawking at me.

What the…?

5

ABBY

I stood still, a statue of a drooling idiot. My brain — already fried from the events of this morning — had completely shut down. First, I'd chased our QB right off school property like a certified crazy person. And then I had almost mowed him down with my car. He hadn't sworn at me or smacked my car's rusted hood — which was lucky, because sometimes that stopped the engine. He just waved, a concerned look in his eyes. Almost like he was more worried about the driver who almost hit him than his own health. Weird.

Then, in a moment worthy of a celebrity trying to prove they're a good person to the paparazzi, he stopped to talk to someone's grandma and help her with her shopping. They'd even laughed together. I mean, come on. This was Chase Jones we were talking about. It was not what I had expected from the person I'd assumed was the prototypical dumb jock.

Maybe you should start checking your assumptions, Abby.

Or maybe he knew I was following him. Maybe he was waiting for me to snap a picture for Click. Nice try, Chase Jones.

"Are you lost?" Chase's voice brought me back to earth. He held an empty wax cup for frozen yogurt.

"Yes. No. Sorry. Long morning." I muttered like a fool. Did he recognize me?

"Imagine how much longer it would've been if you'd ran me over," he said, not unkindly. I could have sworn I even saw a smile playing on his lips. Man, he really was that good looking up close.

I blushed furiously. Yup. He recognized me. "Sorry."

"All good," a real smile this time.

"Why did you run before?" I asked, curiosity still rippling through me.

"Huh?"

"Never mind!" I said quickly. Guess he hadn't heard me yelling before. He had looked preoccupied.

At the smell of freshly baked waffle cones and swirls of sugar, my stomach grumbled. In my morning rush, I'd forgotten to eat breakfast. Normally, I didn't approve of frozen yogurt for breakfast, but this wasn't exactly a normal day, was it? I grabbed a wax cup and took my place beside Chase, who was examining the flavors as if he were trying to dissect a defense.

"Birthday cake," I said. I could almost feel my brain retreating and trying to escape my body. You should prob-ably speak in full sentences, Abby, so you stop sounding like you have a 0 IQ.

Chase raised his eyebrows, a smile on his lips again. "Birthday cake?"

I pointed. "It's the best. Very sweet though. I like to take the edge off with some dark chocolate. Top it with crushed peanut butter cups, and you have the perfect combination."

"A connoisseur." He raised his eyebrows and rubbed his chin. "Do you go for flavor or style?"

"Flavor. One hundred percent. Who goes for style?"

"I tried once," he admitted. "I got the blue raspberry with Swedish Berries and those blue dolphin candies."

"How'd that go?" I looked at him, feeling a bit strange. What a surreal morning.

"The dolphins were so stale I broke a tooth."

"Actually?" *You idiot, Abby. Of course not actually.* He was making a joke. I'd never been this close to Chase before, and I couldn't deny that he had the presence that made me feel slightly clumsy.

He stepped away from the machine that served strawberry and vanilla and took a step towards the one holding birthday cake.

"I'll try your suggestion. But if I don't like it — you have to pay." He grinned.

"If you don't like it, you're wrong."

He looked at me for a second, his face bemused. And then he laughed. Hard, like I had surprised him. The sound warmed my body.

Focus, Abby.

"So. I'm Abigail Murrow. Abby."

"The journalist?"

A thunderbolt of shock hit my face. "You read the Pinnacle?"

He winked. "As long as it's not about me. I'm Chase Jones."

"Obviously." *Abby. What. Are. You. Doing?* "Sorry. I mean. Nice to meet you."

Wow, he had introduced himself instead of assuming I knew his name. This guy was breaking down all of my assumptions.

We finished making our frozen yogurts. When he set his cup on the scale, I put mine beside his and offered to pay, insisting it was the least I could do for him after almost killing him.

"Man, do I look that depressed?" Chase asked.

"You are having frozen yogurt on a Monday morning."

"Excellent point." He smiled. In one swift movement he whipped out his wallet and tapped his card to the machine. Before I'd even touched my wallet.

"My treat," he said, "Least I can do for you after you cheered up my morning."

I'd cheered up Chase Jones's morning?

He was about to take a seat. I had to say something before I lost my nerve. "I was wondering…"

Chase looked at me expectantly.

"I have this article I'm supposed to write. It's about Evermore social life."

His expression darkened, and I recoiled, surprised.

"I'm sorry, it's dumb. Thanks again for the yogurt." I turned to leave, my cheeks red again.

"No, no, don't worry." He said quickly. "Please, it's all good. I was just hoping… ah never mind. What's the article?"

I explained the article, and I told him how, since I did not engage in high school social events myself, I'd decided the best way to go about this project was to interview the popular kids, seeing as Evermore was just one big popularity contest of a school. He flinched when I mentioned he was the first person I had thought of interviewing.

"You hate the idea," I said. His face was easy to read. He looked like I'd replaced his frozen yogurt with soggy asparagus.

I guess cheering up his morning had been a temporary fix.

"I don't love it," he replied slowly. I must have looked crestfallen, because he added "I'm sorry Abby, I could definitely do you an interview about football or something instead?"

I shook my head. "That's Payton Clarence's realm - sports. Look, forget I mentioned it…"

Chase looked at me and again, his eyes were not unkind. They were almost sad, I realized, also realizing simultaneously what a beautiful shade of navy blue they were. "Can you give me some time to think about it? I'm not saying no, I'm just not really in a good head space for deciding right now."

"Totally okay," I said, nodding. This had already gone so differently than I had expected, with Chase buying me yogurt and laughing at my jokes. It somehow didn't shock me when he shied away from the interview request. Honestly, before speaking to him, I had assumed all the popular kids would be so self-obsessed that they would leap at the chance to be the Featured Popular Kid for the school paper. But Chase? Full of surprises, this one.

"I'll let you know."

"Great." I turned to leave, pausing at the door. "I'm sorry I almost hit you with my car."

He laughed grimly. "Thanks, wouldn't want to get run over twice in one day."

I smiled back, not really sure what he meant. That was my first interaction with Chase Jones. And it was safe to say that he was really, truly, absolutely nothing like what I expected.

6

ABBY

a week after nearly taking out our school hero with my car, I was making careful plans to go to my first high school party. Parties were a non-negotiable part of high school for anyone with any kind of social life - i.e. anyone who wasn't me. And as much as I wasn't looking forward to it, I knew I had to bite the bullet and prove my journalistic range to Nicholas and Mr. Adebayo.

It was actually Nicholas who had suggested the party. At school, I'd taken the opportunity to take Nicholas aside to discuss the social feature and get his input. And, to be honest, it was also a GREAT opportunity to spend some alone time with him — even if he was distracted by the blinking cursor on his laptop for most of our conversation. He recommended trying to put myself in the shoes of a typical high school student. What would they experience? What would they look forward to?

His answer: The first party of the year.

Every single year, the first big back-to-school party took place after the Evermore Panther's first home football game of the season, Nicholas informed me.

I looked at him, hopefully. "Are you going?"

Nicholas sighed a rather self-righteous "Oh, no," as he took off his glasses to polish them on his shirt. My fledgling hope dissolved in an instant. It turned out he had a beat poetry reading that night, or else he definitely would have been there, he assured me.

I wasn't super sure if I believed him.

I shrugged off the thought — Nicholas was far too good for these high school parties, anyway. He was mature and worldly, on a fast track to Northwestern next year, his number one college pick. I imagined him leaning forward during round table discussions, eager to contribute to many-an intellectual debate.

Sigh. Only two years to go and I would hopefully be in a similar place.

Since I wasn't much of a social/gossip writer, I decided that I would approach my party feature like the investigative journalist I so desperately wanted to be. I would wear a disguise, the disguise of the cliché high school student. I'd always managed to be invisible, so how hard could it be to blend in?

"You're not serious." Isabel Yang, my best and only friend, sat on the end of my bed on Friday night, groaning dramatically. We had skipped the actual football game as I figured I needed at least a couple of hours to get my look right.

Apparently two hours were not enough. Izzy examined my outfit — the one I hoped would transform me into a popular high schooler — with a critical eye. "You absolutely cannot wear that. They'll think you're a narc."

I glared. "I wish you loved me enough to lie."

I looked at the tight black cocktail dress, hanging skimpily on its hanger. I'd found it in one of the few bags of things that mom didn't take with her when she left us almost two years ago.

The dress was lacy and sheer, a far cry from my usual "casual professional" look that featured a rotation of plaid skirts, oxford shirts, and slacks. My little sister Katie was always laughing at my clothes. "They don't look like you, Abby!" She would tell me. "They look like you are dressing up to make people think a certain way of you!"

Katie may have had a point. My serious image was carefully curated - fashion was surely a distraction, wasn't it? And didn't I want NYU to take me seriously? *Nicholas to take me seriously?*

Isabel laughed and slurped her iced coffee, bringing me back to the present. "Guess I love you too much to lie. Let me work my magic."

She set her cup down and brushed past me, before shifting through my closet. Iz and I have been best friends since the first day of seventh grade. We were both lost, looking for our homeroom, and we had run into each other — literally — in the hallway in our mutual panic. She had a better excuse to be lost than I did: her family had just moved here from LA. My excuse was a little more pathetic. All the other kids had spent their time before the first bell finding their friends. When the bell rang, they moved to class in a flock. Me? I was engrossed in my novel, sitting on the front step of the school. By the time I looked up, the hallways had cleared, and I realized I had no idea where I was going. It was mortifying. I think my hatred of being late formed at that very moment.

Izzy sighed repeatedly as she flicked through my closet. "Abs, we badly need to go shopping. Like stat." She eventually picked out a couple of things she deemed acceptable and shoved the coat hangers into my chest. "These."

I changed, nervously, into a black halter top I had never worn before — the tags were still attached — and a pair of soft, skinny grey jeans that I had gotten as a Christmas present last year from my Aunt Jess in California. I had forgotten I even had them.

I surveyed myself in the mirror as Izzy smiled behind me, holding up the finishing touch she had picked out — a pair of black ankle booties.

I buckled them onto my feet with a glance in Isabel's direction. Fashion came easily to Izzy. Thanks to her petite frame and natural sense of style, everything looked good on her. She was wearing a short babydoll dress and white high-top Converse shoes for the party.

"Ner-vous?" Izzy asked, drawing out the word.

"I just want to be the perfect high school student."

"I don't think that exists." Izzy rolled her eyes as she picked off a piece of lint off my top. "Just be yourself."

"But if I'm not perfect, they won't let me into the party."

"If that was the prerequisite to get in, no one would be there." Izzy threw up her hands. "Trust me Abs, any party that doesn't want to let you in is a party you don't want to go to." Part of me was grateful for Izzy's effortless confidence. The other part of me was jealous. She always knew what to say.

There was a knock on my bedroom door.

"Come in."

The door opened and my dad smiled, poking his head in. My dad and I looked super alike, with the same brown hair and wiry physique, and the same green eyes. I claimed they were colored like emeralds, but he said that I was wrong, and they were actually the color of freshly cut grass. Because every girl wants to hear that their eyes look like someone's lawn.

I groaned when I saw what was in his hand: an old-school Polaroid camera.

"You're joking," I said.

"It's for the album," Dad said. Ever since mom left, he'd

been obsessed with putting together photo albums of our lives for Katie and I. Every moment of my life was documented in a thick binder in our basement. Originally, he'd wanted to start an online album, but my sister and I refused. We did not want embarrassing photos of ourselves plastered on the family Facebook page. Dad's concession was that he got to take as many photos as he wanted, but they stayed offline. We agreed.

"Izzy, get in there too," Dad said.

Izzy threw her arms around me and kicked up her heel, posing for the camera with ease. I forced a smile, wiping my sweaty palms on my jeans.

Flash. Click. And we were off to the party.

I HAD the nervous energy of a six-year-old who'd accidentally drank a pot of coffee. I couldn't hold my hands still if I tried, so I drummed my fingers along the steering wheel repeatedly as I drove Izzy and I to the party.

"Are you sure we're going the right way?" I asked.

"Relax," Izzy said. "You'll be fine."

When you knew someone as well as Izzy and I knew each other, you got used to each other's nervous ticks. Mine was constantly looking for reassurance that I was doing things the right way. If I was baking a cake, I'd check my measurements a hundred times before I poured the flour into the mixing bowl, meaning I wasn't exactly a barrel of laughs to bake red velvet cupcakes with.

I took a left into suburbia, then another left, and we were there. I had found the address thanks to some online sleuthing through students' profiles.

Poorly parked cars packed the street, putting my mind at ease that this was, in fact, the right place. I found an empty spot a few blocks away and pulled into it haphazardly. My driving was not at its best when I was nervous. Izzy and I walked back over towards the party, the heels on my boots clicking with more dread with every step I took. I hated to admit it, but I was nervous. It had been easy for the duration of my high school career to avoid the popular crowd all together and just be invisible. I wanted nothing to do with it. I still didn't, I told myself; I was doing this for my story! Despite trying to reassure myself, the thought of trying and failing, of being rejected… it was really getting to me.

The party was easy to find — all you had to do was follow the thumping bass. Each drum beat tangled my stomach in another knot.

The house was dark, but laughs and shouts came from the backyard. A single red solo cup was lying on the front lawn.

"Backyard," Izzy said, directing me towards a boy standing near a fenced gate.

Calling the mountain that guarded the gate a boy was an understatement. He was probably all of fifteen years old, but he stood well over six feet tall and had a full beard already. I vaguely recognized him as one of the offensive linemen who played for Evermore's JV football team. The thick scent of cheap body spray — undoubtedly named after some natural disaster like Hurricane or Earthquake — clouded the air.

Oh come on, they have the JV guys playing security?

"Hey," I said. What was I supposed to say? Was there a secret password? I looked to Izzy for help.

"We're here for the party," she explained.

"What party?" The boy's voice was gruff.

Izzy cocked her head. "Who put you on guard dog duty? Someone from the varsity team? I didn't think a backyard party needed a bouncer."

"He wants to keep it small. Only football guys and their girls."

"Who does?" I asked, knowing he was lying. There were clearly a ton of people in the backyard, judging by the noise level.

"If you don't know whose party this is, then you're not coming in." Mountain boy raised his eyebrows, challenging us.

Izzy took a step forward, staring up at the giant. "We could hop the fence. You don't look that fast."

"I run a four-nine forty." He crossed his arms, impressed with himself.

Izzy glanced at me, our expressions similar: What the heck did that mean?

I shivered and tried to peer past the giant, but the fence was too tall to see what was going on. Judging from the delighted screams, whatever was happening at the party was more fun than I'd had in a long time. Plus, I smelled campfire, and fire meant warmth. "Can we just do a quick lap?"

The boy sighed, exasperated. I almost felt bad for him for a split millisecond. It's not like he got to go into the party either. "Don't you get it? You're not coming in. So beat it. Find someone else to piss off."

7

CHASE

$\mathcal{I}$ leaned back in the lawn chair and held a bag of crushed ice against my aching shoulder. Tonight's game had been a rough one, starting the season with a bang, and we'd had to fight hard for our narrow win against the Hollyhill Wildcats.

Late in the third quarter, I'd taken a vicious sack. The defensive end landed on me, pressing his full weight on my body. Thanks to a recent rule change, it was a fifteen-yard penalty for roughing the passer, automatic first down. That penalty put us in the red zone, and a play later Dylan caught a pass in the flats and scampered in for the go-ahead touchdown.

Adrenaline carried me through the rest of the game. But after the adrenaline wore off, the pain returned.

I'd grudgingly agreed to come to the after party because Dylan had insisted I didn't have a choice. It was our captain, Adam Zamos' annual back to school bash, and, as he was a senior this year, this one would be his last hurrah. While my shoulder hurt, it wasn't the only discomfort I was dealing with. I hadn't been seeing Savannah long, but I thought we'd grown close in the time we'd spent together. It felt like a missed opportunity, an interception on the goal line. But more than that, I didn't understand why it had happened. It was starting to get under my skin. Three times in a row, dumped exactly three-weeks after Click announced I was seeing someone. It couldn't be a coincidence.

Dylan sat in the chair beside me, cup in his hand. "Dude, you need to let loose. We won. You're the best quarterback in the state. And you still don't look like you're having any fun."

I grimaced and shifted the ice pack. "I'm not the best quarterback in the state."

"You're the only QB I'd want."

"You kidding me? Go get yourself a QB that can't throw and the coach'll give you the ball thirty times a game. That's at least twenty touchdowns. A game." I exaggerated on purpose. Dylan was a phenomenal player, and I was constantly worried he didn't get the recognition he deserved. I would literally be half the quarterback I was if I wasn't able to trust him to pick up a first down on third and short. Or to block a linebacker when they came screaming in on a weak-side blitz.

Dylan laughed. "Dude, you think I'm a lot faster than I am."

Around us, the backyard party was in full swing. Adam grilled a pack of smokies over the firepit, turning them as the grease fell to the embers and sizzled. His girlfriend Hailey Danielson was beside him, still in her cheerleading uniform, and Hailey's best friend — my sister Jordyn — sat on her other side, laughing with Peter Landry, our team's second string QB.

Girls flirted with guys, tossing their hair. Boys puffed out their chests and inflated their accomplishments, talking about their great blocks, their great tackles, their perfect catches. These were the same boys that would be beet red and embarrassed by their mistakes when we watched a game film on Monday.

"Hey, babe," Madison, my ex, was suddenly standing in front of me. I looked up — man, she was looking seriously hot tonight — but I couldn't help but feel completely removed from the situation. She was hot, yes, but it didn't excite me anymore. Not like it used to. Madi still called me "babe" all the time, like she had some claim to me. I never fought it. Madison had a habit of just doing what she wanted at all times, and I was just glad that most of the time what she wanted to do didn't involve me. I heard she had moved on to a freshman at Boulder who had his own YouTube channel. I, for one, was glad. A Youtuber would surely suit her better than I had. He'd at least like the attention more.

"Hey, Madi," I replied, disinterested. I noticed one of the JV guys looking over at me enviously. I knew why: Madison Albright was a big deal at Evermore due to her 30,000 Instagram followers, constant features on Click, and insanely good looks. Everyone — except Jordyn and Dylan — thought I was crazy when I broke up with her. But honestly? I hated the social media. The endless selfies. Our relationship blasted all over Click for the whole high school to see.

Madi scowled, irked I wasn't paying enough attention to her. As if she wasn't getting enough attention from the younger guys. They were drooling so much that the lawn wouldn't need watering for a month.

"Loosen up, Jones, you look like you'd rather be at a funeral." Madi chastised me.

"I know Madi, I know... I'm just so boring, aren't I?" I teased.

"Yes!" she snapped. "You are. And that's exactly why I dumped you!"

I stifled a snort at her skewed version of the truth as she sauntered off. Whatever makes her happy, I guess, I thought, before returning to icing my shoulder. I didn't give it another moment's thought. I knew she would find me in the hallway and say hi to me at school on Monday, as if nothing had happened. It was just Madi's way.

Dylan hadn't been wrong when he said I didn't have a choice to come: my attendance at these backyard football parties was basically mandatory. When you became the starting quarterback, there were certain expectations about how you would act. The expectations came from your team-mates. Your friends. Your teachers. Your coaches. Your community. Everyone wanted you to be everything at all times. I didn't want to complain. That was the part of the job description. If you wanted the glory, you had to live with the grime.

Adam lifted his cup in the air and made a toast. The same one I'd heard a thousand times. We were the best. We would go undefeated. Absolutely nothing could stop us. This was a party for state champions. I remembered this speech. It was the same one I'd heard last year the week before we got bounced from the playoffs.

I held up my water bottle halfheartedly as everyone cheered. A girl I didn't recognize bounced over. Probably a new freshman on the cheerleading team. She twirled a finger through her hair and blinked at me. "Great game, Chase!"

"Thanks," I said.

"Oh my goodness, are you hurt? Do you need anything?" Just like that, she was at my side, her hand on the ice pack. I noticed a flash as someone snapped a picture.

"Just a flesh wound," I said, gently pulling away from her.

She looked confused. "I don't get it. Is that bad?"

"I'm okay."

"Okay. Well, if there's anything, I'm around. It's Kimberly, by the way." She blinked at me again before bouncing back over to her friends, giggling. One of them showed her their phone. I guessed that's where the flash had come from.

"What's it like to be a photo op?" Dylan asked. He finished his drink and balanced the empty cup on the armrest. "The mood you're in tonight, I bet we could replace you with a cardboard cutout and no one would know the difference."

I laughed. "We should try that at the next party. I'll print a picture of my face and staple it to a pillow. Put the jersey on it and everything. You can just say I gained a few pounds."

"You joke, but when the Chase Jones body pillow takes off you're gonna have some serious regrets."

I didn't even want to think about that.

Dylan stretched and yawned. "Wanna head out?"

I nodded. "Definitely."

We said our goodbyes — and patiently listened to the complaints. No! Dylan, Chase, you can't go, it's too early. The party is just getting started. We'll get in trouble without you here to watch over us — as if I was the team's babysitter or something. I indulged my teammates as best I could, then pushed the gate open.

"You're not coming in. So beat it. Find someone else to piss off." The voice belonged to Brett, one of the sophomore guards for the JV team. Adam had told him to post up near the entrance and not let anyone through. Brett had happily obliged. Anything to get in the varsity team captain's' good books, I guess. That was life at Evermore. I rolled my eyes at the very thought. As if a backyard high school football party needed a bouncer.

I was instantly more interested in the situation when I recognized the girl he was talking to — Abby, the weird reporter from the school paper, who was standing there in front of Brett with her hands on her hips. What a strange girl.

I noticed she looked cute, though. Different from when

39

I'd run into her at Peak's. For the first time since the game ended, I felt something besides pain. I was genuinely curious: Why was she here? This wasn't her scene.

She spotted me and her lips parted, but she said nothing. It was probably for the best. I was tired and definitely not up to do an interview right now.

I smiled. "Did you run over anyone on your way here?"

Her face split in a grin. "I was waiting for you. Thought if I caught you on a dark road I'd have a better chance of taking you out."

I laughed. She really was cute, I realized, with that dimpled smile and sparkly green eyes. I motioned towards Brett. "He giving you guys a tough time?"

Brett's fearsome demeanor dissolved into that of a frightened child. "Oh, man, sorry, I didn't know. Yeah, sorry, you should've said you were with Jones, yeah, sorry. Sorry."

"All good, my man." I gave him a fist bump, then nodded to Abby and her friend. "A couple of spots just opened up by the fire. Enjoy the party."

Her friend looked to Abby, then to me, then back to Abby, clearly confused.

Abby eyed the ice pack on my shoulder. "Rough night?" she raised her eyebrows.

I nodded my head to Dylan. "This guy forgot to pick up a blitz."

"And he'll never let me live it down," Dylan said, smiling.

"How bad is it?" Abby asked. "I wasn't at the game. I went looking for my school spirit but I couldn't find it."

Of course she wasn't at the game. This chick was one of those girls who danced to the beat of her own drum. She was probably the only girl in the junior class who hadn't been there.

"Nothing I can't walk off." I grinned at her.

"I'd hate to have you knocked out for the season before

our interview," Abby said. Man, she was relentless. She flashed me what I'm sure she thought was a winning smile. "Glad to hear it's just a flesh wound."

For a second brief moment, the pain in my shoulder vanished as I eyed Abigail Murrow with interest. She wasn't like any other girl at our school, it seemed.

"Have a good night." I said, meaning it.

"You too," she looked away without her gaze lingering.

Dylan and I left the girls standing by the fence. He continued our previous conversation immediately, as if nothing had happened. "This whole thing with Savannah is weird."

"You're telling me."

"Like, dude. Another girl breaks up with you exactly three weeks after your blasted on Click? If I didn't know any better, I'd say you were cursed. Or you've got one vindictive ex-girlfriend."

Well, that much we knew was true.

8

ABBY

ver the summer, I read countless articles and stories by the investigative journalists I longed to call my peers. Inevitably, the question would come up time after time: if you wanted to be a journalist, what was the most important skill to develop? And the answer was always the same — you needed to hone your instincts, so you knew when to keep digging.

As I laid in my bed on Friday night, my heavy comforter squishing me in place, my instincts were shouting. Before our short-lived appearance at the backyard party — where we clearly weren't welcome — I'd overheard Dylan Ramirez mention that multiple girls had broken up with Chase Jones exactly three weeks after their relationship was put on Click. High school relationships were almost always short-lived... but for consecutive relationships to end at the exact same time? Was that what he was so upset about on Monday at Peak's? That this Savannah girl had broken up with him?

Something was going on.

Izzy laid beside me, her eyes closed. She was already half asleep, but I was wide awake, my mind running at full speed.

"What do you think?" I asked. "It's weird, right? Three weeks, every time?"

"I think you're thinking too hard." She yawned. "And that you should just let this go. I've seen guys get dumped because they didn't text their girlfriend every morning."

"But three weeks to the day... and this is Chase Jones we are talking about. Not some randos who never text their girlfriends back."

"It probably wasn't three weeks exactly," Izzy said sleepily. "Boys don't remember dates... and since when do you care about Chase Jones? And how do you know him, anyway? You never explained."

Maybe Izzy was right. But while she was about to pass out into a blissful sleep, my instincts were running in overdrive. I rolled onto my side and stared at my window. Streaks of orange streetlight filtered through the blinds. There were a handful of glow-in-the-dark stars still stuck to my wall. When I was little, I'd desperately wanted to decorate my ceiling with those Dollar Store stars. I even drew a map with all the constellations I wanted. But when I approached my parents with my plan, my mom refused. She didn't want to wreck the paint. When she left, I'd bought the stars and put them up as a small act of rebellion, even though I was way too old to have neon stars on my ceiling. Ironically, all they did was remind me of her.

"But what if it was three weeks exactly?" I said, pushing the thoughts of my mom from my mind.

Izzy snorted awake. "Are you still on this? Maybe there's just something wrong with him. And it takes three weeks to figure it out."

"He dated Madison Albright for some of freshman year and then most of sophomore year," I pointed out.

Chase and Madison's relationship — and subsequent break up — was all anyone had talked about for weeks last spring. Click overflowed with rumors and lies. Somewhere in the swirl of speculation, the truth hid. I didn't investigate that mystery. Madison would rip my head from my body if I tried to talk to her. I shuddered, remembering the disgusted look she had shot me earlier in the night, as I had walked into the backyard party. "What if Dylan is right? What if something else is going on?"

"Not your circus, not your monkeys."

She was right. If — and it was a big if — something was going on in Chase's love life, that was his problem. But his friendliness was also the only reason we could get into the party this evening for our three minutes of terror. There's nothing like walking into a party where you literally know no one. I'd never felt so uncomfortable. If Chase had stayed, that would've been one thing. At least I felt like I could talk to him.

Not that he would have talked to me, I reminded myself. I'm sure everyone wanted to talk to Chase Jones at every party.

An idea popped in my head.

"What if it was my circus?"

Izzy groaned and smothered herself with a pillow.

"Seriously!" I said, excitement bubbling in my voice. "There might be something wrong with Chase, or maybe someone is sabotaging his love life. If there's something wrong with him, no one will tell him, because he's the star quarterback. And if someone is sabotaging him, he will never know. But what if he could know?"

"Why don't you sleep on it?" Izzy said from beneath her pillow.

"I could tell him. I could help him find out."

She lifted the pillow from her face. "You sound crazy right now. What are you going to do, start by stalking anyone he dates to look for suspicious behavior?" she asked sarcastically.

I sat up with a start. "YES! Great idea, Izzy!"

"It was NOT an idea, I was being sarcastic, you creeper. Anyway, what about your paper editor, He of the Dreamy Cheekbones? Surely it won't be great for your chances with him if you get muddled up in the love life of Chase Jones, of all people."

"That makes it even more perfect." I couldn't contain my excitement. "I help Chase find out why he's being dumped. He can repay me by getting me into all the best parties and help me live out the cliché high school life. What better vantage point is there for the social feature than tagging along with the quarterback? Then, when I'm done, I'll have loads of material and I'll be able to write an amazing story. Which will impress Nicholas so much that he'll be dying to discuss it with me. Maybe over dinner?"

"Have you considered just telling Nicholas you like him?"

The very idea nearly gave me a heart attack. "My plan is much better."

"Abs. I love you. And you know I hate to use the word insane. But… you're insane."

"It's foolproof."

"You're insane," Izzy repeated. "And you're also forgetting something. Yes, ok, so Chase Jones was nice to you tonight… but do you really think he would be up for you digging into his love life?"

Isabel had a point.

9

CHASE

$\mathcal{I}$ plunged my spoon into a bowl of frozen yogurt — birthday cake mixed with dark chocolate, topped with crushed peanut butter cups — and tried to calm my nerves. Abby, the strange, intrepid wannabe journalist that she was, had cornered me on my way to practice and asked me again for an interview, telling me we could meet here after my practice was over. Normally, school reporters just asked me a handful of questions while I stood on the side-lines with a dixie cup of Gatorade.

But not Abby. She had worn me down to do the interview in the first place by assuring me we would focus mainly on football.

"Didn't you say sports were Payton's thing?" I eyed her warily, but she laughed it off.

"Oh yes, but today, it's mine!" And then she insisted we meet for frozen yogurt.

"I want to see Chase Jones out of his element," she said, squinting against the late afternoon sun. "And besides, if we get froyo, I can expense it."

I regretted that I'd ever conceded to the interview in the first place as she looked at me expectantly.

"The Pinnacle has an expense account?" As soon as the words left my mouth, I regretted them. It was a joke. *Way to play up to the dumb jock stereotype, Jones.*

"See you after practice?" she asked.

I sat on a bench outside of Peak's as I waited. My legs were jumpy, my feet nervously tapping the brick. Main Street was packed. It felt like the entire town had taken advantage of our unusually warm September.

I was midway through my bowl of frozen yogurt when Abby arrived. She looked — for lack of a better term — smart. Different than she had looked at the party the other night. She carried a notepad that was covered with blue ink.

"Please tell me you don't have an entire page of questions for me."

She grinned. "Double-sided. And I was meant to be buying your yogurt this time around."

"I don't know if I have enough stock answers for you." When you gave enough interviews, you developed routine answers for the questions reporters typically threw your way. Team played well tonight. We executed. Good game plan. Was nice to hear the crowd. Stuff like that.

Abby sat beside me with an enormous smile, her eyes wide. "So. Shall we discuss your deepest and darkest secrets?"

Why did I ever say yes to this strange, persistent girl?

10

ABBY

*T*he interview was going well. As long as I was in reporter mode, I wasn't too nervous around Chase.

He was a great interviewee and put me at ease immediately. I couldn't believe how easy he was to chat with. He had a calm, pleasant demeanor, and he made me laugh. Even better, I made him laugh. Repeatedly.

I noticed he was tapping his foot... nervously? I wasn't sure why he would be nervous, but either way, I did my best to put him at ease, too. I could sense he wasn't a fan of interviews and I was also painfully aware that I wasn't sure why he had agreed to this in the first place, when interviews clearly weren't his thing.

I reassured him the interview would be mainly about sports, so I started with sports to get him talking. He was more than willing to chat about football and was always quick to give credit to his teammates. He talked carefully, thinking about every word before he said it, which made it difficult to skew him towards saying anything that would be at home in the social feature. I got a slight popularity angle for my piece as he talked about the pressure he felt being the quarterback for the varsity team. The only real hiccup came when I asked him about his family. He joked that he thought the story was supposed to be about football, but I could sense that he was putting his shields up. I decided not to push him. Not everyone was comfortable talking about their family life. I, for one, certainly wasn't.

As the interview neared its end, my own nerves returned.

Chase took my empty yogurt bowl from me and tossed it in the recycling bin. He rubbed his throat. "I think that's the most I've talked all week."

"And all I had to do to get you to open up was almost hit you with my car."

He gave me an earnest look and put his hand on his heart. "I take threats against my life very seriously."

"As you should. I'm incredibly dangerous."

Chase laughed, and his navy-blue eyes sparkled. The sound was infectious.

"Well, thanks for choosing me to interview. I hope I was a worthy subject," he said.

Oh no. He was wrapping things up and I hadn't brought up my plan. "Wait," I said. "There's something I wanted to talk to you about."

He raised his eyebrows, but said nothing.

"Off the record." I assured him.

He folded his arms and looked at me curiously, still saying nothing. I took a massive deep breath and proceeded.

"When we were at the party, I overheard Dylan. He said you've been getting dumped a lot." Oh, Abby. There were about a thousand better ways to start this conversation. "Not that it's your fault, I'm sure."

"This isn't going in the article, is it?" I saw the betrayal flash through his eyes immediately, all of his walls suddenly up.

"No. Completely off the record. I'm a woman of my word."

He looked uncertain, guarded.

"I promise." In slight desperation I offered him my pinky, like I was eight years old or something.

He suddenly laughed. "You might be the weirdest reporter I've met."

"I take that as a compliment!" I said, and he laughed again.

And then, by some miracle, he reached out and locked his pinky with mine, casually bumping our fists together.

"You could say I've had some bad luck." He suddenly looked tired. "But nothing you need to worry about, seriously. Thanks for the… concern. Or whatever it was."

"What if it was more than bad luck?" I pressed.

"Do you know something?" He suddenly looked suspicious again.

"No," I admitted. "But I might be able to find out."

"How?"

"I could ask around. People might tell me things they won't tell you."

He considered this. "And what's in it for you?"

"Access," I said. There wasn't much point in sugarcoating it. "I want to be the senior editor of the Pinnacle next year. To do that, I need to kill it with this social feature. Which means I need to get into all the cool high school events. And well… you saw how well that went at the party. People aren't exactly lining up to invite me to things."

Chase nodded slowly, taking my words in.

"So, if we go together…"

He exhaled slowly, his cheeks puffing out like a blowfish. "I see. Well, my first thought is that it sounds crazy."

We watched a pair of young lovers walk by, their hands intertwined.

"And my second thought is that the last person I want to trust with my personal life is someone that could make a public story about it."

I protested, but he cut me off.

"You seem really nice, but I barely know you," Chase said. "And my whole private life going public thing? I've been burned by Click before."

"It's not like I know you much better," I replied. "And I have zero desire to get involved in your business or meddle with it. All I want to do is investigate for you, and all I want you to do for me is get me into some parties. It's a fair trade."

Chase ran his hand through his hair. "Look, you're a cool girl. But I still like Savannah. What if people think we're dating? What if she thinks we're dating?"

Did he just call me cool? I considered his question. "If Savannah asks, just deny, deny, deny. It will be the truth. Plus, if people think we're dating, that's even better — if someone is sabotaging you, and they think I'm your girl-friend, then…"

"They'll come after you." He finished.

"And I'll be able to tell you everything they're doing." I sat up straight and stared ahead. I was proud of my plan, but I didn't have the nerve to look Chase in the eye. He remained quiet.

This had to work. It was my only chance.

I thought he might be trying to work out if I was insane or not for a second, and then I realized what the problem might be. "Chase, I am not trying to date you. Unlike every single other girl at Evermore High, I don't want to go out with you, ok? I mean you're nice and everything…"

I looked at him and saw he was staring at me, incredulously. I guessed no girls were ever so upfront with him, so I bit the bullet and continued. "Look, if we're being honest, I have a crush on someone too."

"Who's that?" When I didn't answer immediately, he added, "strictly off the record."

"Nicholas Applebee. He's a senior."

"Never heard of him."

"He's the senior editor. He gave me the social feature. If I do a good job and impress him with it…"

"Huh." Chase bit his lip, pondering. "I don't think we can do this. Not if we only go halfway."

It was my turn to look confused. "What do you mean?"

He leaned forward, his voice hushed. "You're right. If people think we're dating, and someone's after me, they'll come after you. And they'll let you into the parties. So, we go all the way. You pretend you're my girlfriend. We get blasted on Click. Then, three weeks later, we find out if something is really going on. While we're waiting, I'll get you into any social event you want access to. Then, when it's all over, we both explain it to Savannah. You get your social feature, I get the girl. Everyone wins."

Chase Jones was willing to pretend that I, Abigail Murrow, was his actual girlfriend? Whoa. This was all starting to feel surreal.

"Nicholas might even notice me more if I have a boyfriend," I agreed, slowly collecting my thoughts. "Maybe I could use this as a reason to make him jealous."

"Right. We work together. You figure out why I can't keep a girl I like, I get you into the events you want to write about. I get Savannah back, you impress Nicholas. Strictly business. No feelings involved."

"No feelings involved," I agreed. "And nobody can EVER know."

"Never," he echoed.

I nodded, and Chase stuck out his hand, laughing. "Then let's do it. Abigail Murrow?"

"Yes?"

"Will you be my fake girlfriend?"

11

ABBY

I sat alone on the bleachers, my jacket pulled tight around my shoulders to protect from the wind, my hands folded in my lap. The football field below me was a bright shade of green — the same shade as my eyes, I'm sure my dad would say — and the grounds crew was painting white yard lines. It was early evening, two days after Chase and I had made our bizarre pact.

I had spent two almost sleepless nights reliving the impossible conversation we'd had outside Peak's, playing it over and over in my head. It didn't seem real, and yet it was. I would be Chase Jones's new girlfriend.

Well, fake girlfriend.

But nobody else would know that bit.

The thought was strange. I had never been anyone's girl-friend before, never mind the girlfriend of the boy everyone wanted to date.

And I didn't want Chase to know that I'd never had a boyfriend before. That would need to stay my secret. I felt like I knew him well enough at this point that he would never go for it if he thought he was taking away that first from me. He really seemed to be kind and thoughtful. Two things I had wrongly judged him about previously.

I decided we needed to lay everything out on paper, like any good journalist would do: get the story straight.

So here I was. Chase finished practice a half hour ago, and I was waiting for him. We hadn't announced our "relationship" to anyone yet — there were still a few i's to dot and t's to cross.

Chase emerged from the tunnel that led out from the Athletics Building and jogged across the field, stopping briefly to crack a joke with one groundskeeper. The metal bleachers creaked as he slid into the seat next to me. His dark hair was still wet from the shower, flopping down around his eyes, and he smelled like clean laundry. His t-shirt was damp and stuck to his body, making it way too easy to imagine what he'd look like without it...

I blushed - focus, Abby! - and looked to the mountains in the distance. This was strictly business. "So. We need to discuss our terms and conditions."

A hint of amusement appeared on his face, his deep blue eyes dancing. "Straight to business, huh? I don't even get to ask my new girlfriend how her day was?"

I couldn't tell if he was laughing at me or trying to crack a joke, so I ploughed ahead. "No feelings allowed in this relationship."

"Sounds like my parents' marriage."

I laughed, but again, I couldn't tell if he was joking or not, so I stopped quickly.

I tried to compose myself, then pulled out my notepad and flipped to an open page. "For you, it's easy. My job is to find out why you can't get a girlfriend."

"Whoa. I can get a girlfriend." He said, an exaggerated look of mock hurt on his face.

"Sorry." I cleared my throat. "My job is to find out why you can't keep a girlfriend."

"Yeah 'cause that's so much better," he said sarcastically.

"I'm a journalist, I deal with facts" I told him, as I scribbled into my notepad: Find out why Chase can't keep a girlfriend. I underlined the word keep. "Simple enough. Your job is more complex."

"Nah — I get it. I take you to parties as my girlfriend. We act like girlfriend and boyfriend in public. You get your stories for the paper. It's not rocket science."

"Going to a few football parties won't be enough for the social feature. It's supposed to be an all-encompassing look into the social lives of students at Evermore High. The ultimate undercover expose, if you will."

"I get to read it before you publish it." He tapped my notepad. "Write that down. That one's important."

"Why?"

"Because I'm bringing you into this world. You might see some things. Can't have you trashing all of my friends."

"As long as I can trash you," I joked.

"I'm used to it." He wasn't joking.

"I won't... trash you that is." I told him, suddenly regretting my joke.

I wrote it down: Chase gets to read the article before submission.

"Thanks," he said.

"For this to work for me, I need the full high school experience. I've prepared a checklist."

He laughed. Then he saw my expression. "You're serious?"

"How else would I do this?"

"Abby you are so...." he looked at me strangely, as if no amount of searching could find the word to describe me. "Different."

All the words in the world, and he had settled with different. Great.

"Let me see that." Before I could protest, he snatched my notebook away from me. When I reached to grab it back, he dodged, his reflexes much sharper than mine.

Clearing his throat, he read aloud: "Number one. Go to a football party. Wait, last weekend doesn't count?"

"I felt awkward. We didn't stay."

He shrugged. "Fair enough. Number two. Go to the Costume Crawl on Main." There was a note of confusion in his voice. "You know you don't need me for that one, right? Literally anyone can go. It's a public event."

The Costume Crawl was a Halloween tradition in our town - everybody gathered in full costume on Main Street for the festivities. At Evermore, it was often the time where people first stepped out in public as couples, in cute matching costumes, ready to end up all over Click's gossip blasts the next morning.

"It's not the same if it's just me and Izzy." I tossed him my pen. "Write that down — Izzy gets to come with us."

"Do I have to bring a fake boyfriend for her too?"

"Your call." I raised my eyebrows and fixed him with an even stare.

Chase scribbled something into the notepad before continuing to read. "Number three. Get a public Christmas Crush invite. I don't know…"

I blushed furiously. The Christmas Crush was THE high school event of the fall semester. It was a formal dance that was legendary for guys inviting girls in a lavish, public manner. The spectacle would go on for weeks each November in the hallways of Evermore High. What's more — if the legends were to be believed — the Christmas Crush had the most amazing afterparty. The afterparty was super-secret and by invitation only. If you asked anyone about it, they would deny its very existence. I had never been invited to the afterparty. In fact, I'd never even been invited to the dance itself.

"You don't have to take me to the dance, or the afterparty," I blurted. "But I want the invite."

"The public invite," he corrected, frowning.

"It's important."

"Why?" he seemed genuinely curious now.

Oh, to have never had a single problem getting in anywhere. "For the social feature."

"You said that if this was going to work, we needed to be honest with each other."

Ugh. "Fine. I want the invite because this might be my only chance to get one. I've never been asked to a dance before. I'm not exactly Ms. Popularity at school."

"Wait, you've never been invited to a dance at all. Like any dance?" Chase stared at me like I was an alien.

I blushed furiously and was immediately angry with myself for blushing, for caring at all, which made me redder still.

"No," I admitted, keeping my head up and returning his stare defiantly.

"Well, that will need to change," Chase stated, like it was just a simple fact that could easily be resolved. "What about your guy?"

"Nicholas? He's not my guy." I folded my arms across my chest defensively. "I doubt I'll have impressed him enough to merit an invitation by then. And he's a senior, he'll be gone next year. So even if it works out, I still won't get an invite next year."

"You think pretty far ahead."

Finally, Chase was close enough for me to grab the notepad. I lunged and snatched it back, then furiously scribbled out the invite. "It's fine."

"Hey, it's all good. If you're still my fake girlfriend come November, I'll do an invite for you. And I'll make sure it blows your mind."

He seemed sincere, and I smiled, gratified. Until he added, "Remember, though, we may have this thing wrapped up in three weeks."

He was already counting down the days. I tried to hide my blush by scratching my cheeks. Was I just going to be blushing permanently from now on?

"And that just leaves one more thing. Number four. I need to go on the cliché high school student date."

He looked at me again like I was a brain teaser puzzle that was getting the better of him. "Hang on… You've never been asked to a high school dance… and never been on a high school date?"

Ugh, there was no point in even trying to disguise my blush at this point. I was sure that if Chase found out the truth, he would back out.

So I took a deep breath, looked him dead in the eye, and I lied. "Correct. I have never gone to a high school dance or on a clichéd high school date because I choose to stay away from Evermore social functions. I prefer to date outside school."

The lie slid out of my mouth easily, but I felt funny in my stomach as I watched the look of relief cross Chase's face. If only he knew…

"Ok, easy, I'm glad you think I'm the person to fulfill all the high school clichés for you, as you're too good for them in real life!" His voice dripped sarcasm, but he smiled, making it clear he was kidding with me.

I raised my eyebrows in surprise. I'd expected some resistance.

"Strictly business," Chase said. "I'll walk you through the motions of every last cliché you ever heard of. Besides, if I'm your fake boyfriend, the least I can do is take you out on a fake date. But I'm telling you now — it's dinner and a movie."

"Deal," I replied.

Chase considered this for a moment. He chuckled.

"What?" I asked.

"It's just funny," he said. "I spend way too much time trying to make sure the people around me aren't using me for things. And here I am with you, making a deal so you can use me."

I did not appreciate his phrasing. "You're using me just as much as I'm using you."

He must have caught the tone in my voice. "You're right. My bad. Just... the irony."

I always appreciated irony.

"Oh, one last thing," I said, suddenly feeling shy. I held out my cellphone to Chase. "I guess, if we are going to be a couple, we probably need each other's numbers."

"Yeah," Chase took my phone from my hand and punched in his number, "I'll send a text to myself so I have yours, too."

His phone vibrated, and I nodded curtly, trying to look all business.

He glanced at me again for a second. "Do you think people will, you know, buy it?"

"Buy what?" I asked, my heart suddenly pounding. I couldn't have him bailing at the last hurdle!

"You know, you and me? That we are a... thing?"

The awkwardness in Chase's tone hung in the air between us.

I wasn't stupid. What he ACTUALLY meant was: will anyone ever believe that I would date you?

He was just too nice to say it. And he had a point. Would anyone believe this could happen?

"Don't worry about it," I said crisply, trying to keep my face neutral. "If you need me to do the full Madison Albright makeover for this to be in any way believable, I will oblige. It's part of playing the part."

Chase looked stricken. "No, no, Abby... I didn't mean... that." His tone implied that he did, indeed, mean that.

He ran his hands through his hair as he spoke, "I don't need — or want — for you to look or be anything like Madi, ok?"

I didn't quite believe him.

"Don't change yourself for me, or anyone, Abby — fake or not." He looked at me sincerely for a moment before breaking into a grin. "Just maybe... I dunno... stop dressing like a divorcee stuck in an office job?"

He vaguely gestured toward my blue button-down oxford shirt and black slacks, and despite myself, I laughed. He had a point.

I kept my voice cool and replied. "Noted, Jones. Less business, more bimbo. Especially for you."

I held my breath as I met his stare defiantly.

He frowned, then burst out laughing.

I breathed a long sigh of relief. He was still in.

I scribbled my signature at the bottom of the paper, drew a blank line, and handed the notepad to Chase. "Sign here and we can get started."

He signed, rolling his eyes. "Should we make a prenup for our future fake marriage, too?"

I ignored him and took the notepad back, checked the signature, and stood.

It was official. We were fake dating.

Chase Jones, unbeknownst to him, had just become my first boyfriend of my entire life.

So much for starting our "relationship" with total honesty.

12

ABBY

*T*here was nothing more exciting than preparing to investigate a new story. Normally, I tried to unravel local scandals and unearth the secrets buried by history. But today I'd started working on a new type of investigation: uncovering why Chase Jones couldn't keep a girlfriend for longer than three weeks.

The late September weather was still warm, so I took up residence on the patio in our backyard. The tree in our backyard, a towering Rocky Mountain Maple, was changing color from green to red. I loved the feeling of fall settling into our yard. I'd always thought of fall as a romantic season, and this year, I had a fake boyfriend to share the season with.

I connected my phone to Spotify and turned on my Discover the Mysterious playlist. I made notes.

The facts were:

Ever since Chase's break up with Madison Albright last year, he could not keep a girlfriend for longer than three weeks. In fact, the girls broke up with him on that exact day, three weeks after they were first featured on Click together, every single time.

There were three girls who had dumped Chase Jones:

Phoebe Summers, who was on the soccer team.

Ella Cates, who went to the private school across town.

And finally, Savannah Mayhew, an Evermore senior who was working her way towards a scholarship for dance.

Chase mentioned that before these three relationships, he had never been dumped before. He dated Madison Albright, queen bee of Evermore's social hierarchy, for almost a year before they broke up. Was she his first love?

At the time of their breakup, rumors flooded the corridors of Evermore — the unsurprising fallout of the nuclear detonation that was their demise. The most popular theory was that Chase dumped Madison, so she blasted him on social media and tried to make it look like she dumped him. Knowing how media-shy Chase was, the rumor seemed plausible.

So. Where to start?

I texted Chase.

Abby: Phoebe, Ella, or Savannah. Who should I start with?

Chase: Normal people start conversations with hello.

Abby: Hello. Who should I start with?

Chase: I dunno.

Abby: Helpful much? Come on, I need a lead to go off.

Chase: The only thing I know is that the day we broke up, each of them was acting weird. Not weird like you. Different weird.

Abby: Define different weird. Like I'm gonna break up with you weird?

Chase: Weird. Like they were sad or something.

Abby: Did they say anything unusual?

Chase: Dunno. Don't really remember with the first two tbh. Savannah kept it short. I asked her why but she just said

63

sorry and ran off. Haven't talked to her since. They were all over in like thirty seconds.

Interesting. I appreciated not wanting a long, drawn out break up. But for three girls — all of whom had been super interested in Chase — to break up with him on the same day, in the same general fashion, then refusing to talk to him after? It was very, very suspicious.

Chase: Is that enough of a lead for you?

Abby: I think so. Talk later.

Chase: Wait. You're gonna be my gf and I don't know anything about you. Besides that you're nosy and persistent with a touch of weird.

Abby: Do you call all your girlfriends nosy, persistent, and weird?

Chase: Yes. So, what are you into, Abby Murrow? Fave food?

Abby: Easy, kettle corn. Yours?

Chase: Tacos. Fave thing to do?

Abby: You are officially fake dating Colorado's number one fan of B-Movie slasher flicks. The gorier the better.

Chase: Oh man, horror movies? WHY?

Abby: Scared?

Chase: Terrified.

Abby: I'll protect you. It's that or we have to call the whole thing off.

Chase: You are so weird.

Abby: I try.

The patio door opened. Dad came out carrying a tray with iced tea and store-bought cinnamon buns. He set the tray down. "Even for a teenager, you sure are smiling at your phone a lot."

Busted.

"Are you looking at one of those *me mes*?" Dad asked.

"Memes," I corrected. "And no, I'm talking to a friend

about a project." It felt weird calling Chase Jones a friend. A few weeks ago, we'd never spoken.

"What's Izzy doing?"

"Don't know, maybe you should ask her." I sipped on my iced tea. "I have more than one friend, you know."

"And who's this new friend?"

"His name's Chase."

Dad crossed his arms and nodded, considering this information. Dating had never, ever come up in my social life — this might have been the first time I mentioned a boy to him.

"So, does this Chase play football?" Oh great. Chase Jones was so famous in our town that even my dad had heard of him. Ugh.

"Maybe." I answered carefully.

"Uh-huh," Dad said. "And how do you feel about this Chase?"

"I am feeling that we are not having this conversation," I said. "He's literally just a friend. That's all. And I'm not even interested in Chase, I like—"

I stopped myself. Dad meant well. He was not the type to wait on the front porch with a shotgun if his daughter went out with a boy. Still, it felt weird to talk to him about boys. It felt weird talking to anyone about boys, because I literally knew nothing about them at all.

I had tried talking to my mom about a boy once, back in eighth grade when I'd had a crush on a boy from Model U.N. She'd only cared about his grades and prospective careers.

Maybe Dad would do better. I decided to give it a shot. "There's a boy named Nicholas. He's the senior editor of the Pinnacle. He's the one I like."

"But I thought you were texting with Chase?"

"Just for a school project."

"Must be a fun project. You sure looked happy."

"He's just a friend," I said. "I am definitely not Chase's

type. He only dates the popular girls... you know, perfect cheerleaders and people like that."

"I think you're perfect."

"You're my dad. You're obligated."

"True."

I swatted at him.

"You're not supposed to admit it!" I shrieked, giggling.

"Well, I guess I'm not perfect," he said with a smile.

There was a comfortable silence between us as I devoured my cinnamon bun, using the dough to mop up the cream cheese icing. There was something that had been bugging me and now seemed as good a time as any to bring it up. "Can we have decorations for Christmas this year?"

The corner of his mouth twitched. "I'll think about it."

It may have only been September, but Christmas was already on my mind for good reason. Christmas decorations had been a constant point of contention back when Mom was around. She said that they made the house look messy. We put up a fake tree, but we weren't allowed to decorate it with anything but white Christmas lights because they provided a "clean, modern" look. Last Christmas had been the first year it was just Dad, Katie and me. I had hoped that Dad would have taken initiative to decorate, but instead he'd spent most of the holidays trying to hide his misery. It was heartbreaking.

"Thanks, Dad." I gave him a hug and left.

13

ABBY

*W*hen Monday came, I was wired with excitement. It was the energy that only showed when you were chasing down a lead. I imagined it was the thrill detectives got when they were trying to solve a case and were tracking down potential suspects.

Not only that, it would be my first official day at Evermore as Chase Jones's fake girlfriend. I wondered how that would go and decided I would wait for him to approach me at school. Stupidly, I hadn't thought of making a game plan for our first public interaction, so I guessed we would have to improvise.

I'd dressed up for the momentous occasion, though. Or down, depending on which way you were looking at it. True to my word to Chase, I had ditched my journalism wardrobe and instead wore leggings and a cute white sweater, paired with my favorite baby pink Nike sneakers. I'd also left my hair in long, loose waves, instead of scraping it back in its usual severe ponytail. I had been instantly gratified with the success of this loose hair technique when Nicholas Applebee had done a double take in the hallway as I walked past him this morning. *Score one for Abby!*

I liked my fresh look, it felt very freeing to not be all dressed up like I was playing a part. Now all I had to do was get through the day without spilling something on myself.

Feeling powerful, I snuck out of my first class — History, bleh — early. The teacher was too busy trying to fix a broken globe to notice. I crossed campus, enjoying the blossoming fall colors and the crisp mountain air, and entered the Fine Arts Building I knew so well. But instead of heading to the Pinnacle office, I lounged outside one of the dance studios and pretended to check my phone.

Inside, feet scuffled as the instructor shouted instructions over upbeat music. Soon after, casual applause marked the end of class. The door opened and dancers filed into the hallway, most of them headed to the locker rooms to change. The last girl to leave had long red hair that she'd tied in a ponytail. Her cheeks were flushed, and she was panting.

"Savannah?" Up close, I was instantly taken aback by how pretty she was, with wide blue eyes, full lips, and flawless pale skin.

My hand instinctively flew to my chin, where a developing zit was threatening to need its own zip code very soon. *Sigh.*

Savannah glanced at me. "Hi?"

"Abigail Murrow. I'm with the Pinnacle."

She shook my hand, still confused.

"I wanted to talk to you about something, do you have a minute?"

She checked the time on her phone and shrugged before leading me into the studio. It smelled like a strange mixture of perfume, deodorant, and sweat. There were gigantic bay windows which faced the distant mountains, snow-capped for the first time this year.

I closed the door behind me.

"Is this for the paper?" Savannah asked.

"Exactly," I said, giving her a smile I hoped showed a perfect combination of professionalism and friendliness. "I'm doing a major feature on the social lives of students at Evermore. Right now I'm just gathering material — interviewing people, checking out some stories, seeing what people think. I'd like to ask you a few questions, if that's okay?"

Savannah looked at me uncertainly. "Why me?"

"Why not you? The dance classes are popular and so are the dancers. I bet you have boys all over you." Savannah's eyebrows shot up. Oof. I knew that was the wrong thing to say as soon as the words left my mouth. I sounded like an awkward aunt at a family dinner.

I backtracked quickly. "What I *meant* to say was that I need to get all sides of this story. Someone mentioned you might be a good person to talk to."

She crossed her arms. She wasn't letting me get away that easily. "Who?"

"Dylan Ramirez," I lied. I was positive that if I mentioned Chase's name, she'd run. She already looked skittish.

"Oh."

"Right," I said. "So, what does popularity mean to you?"

Now she was truly stumped. Good. I'd spent my entire weekend thinking of how cleverly I could work my way through this conversation to find out what I needed to know, but I had not thought about my lack of social skills in my planning of this. I needed time to think.

Savannah stumbled over the question, rambling on about how people get featured on Click and then digressing into a vague, humble answer. "What is popularity really? Everyone should just get along and do what makes them happy."

It was the vanilla answer an athlete reserves for the post-game interview when they don't want to get in trouble. The answer Chase would give. The answer Nicholas wouldn't accept.

"Perfect," I said.

Savannah eyed the door. "Is that it?"

"One more thing," I said. She would give nothing away without being pressed. I appreciated that. Too many people spilled their lives all over social media. It was refreshing to meet someone with the presence of mind to stay guarded. "But this is off the record."

She was staring at me strangely — people did that a lot lately — but she nodded for me to continue.

"You were dating Chase Jones, right?"

"I need to go." Savannah grabbed her bag and made for the door.

"It's not like that," I said, "I just don't get it. He's hot. He's nice. And he's the quarterback. As far as popularity goes, he's probably the most popular guy at Evermore. Why dump him?"

"I don't think that's any of your business." Her tone was icy.

This was going nowhere. "Sorry."

Savannah paused, her hand on the door. She sighed. "Why do you want to know this, anyway?"

I didn't know what to say.

She filled the silence for me. "Do you have a crush on Chase? You want to go out with him? Is this what this is all really about?"

"Um…"

She faced me, a sad smile on her beautiful face. "Look, I don't blame you. Everyone wants to be with Chase. I sure did. But being with him in reality, it's not what you expect. It gets complicated."

I leaned forward, intrigued. "How? He likes you, you like him, seems simple to me."

"He still likes me? You talk to him?" Her voice was laced with what sounded like hope.

"I'm profiling him for the social feature." I told her.

"Of course you are. Look... Abby was it?"

I nodded.

"Ok, well, here's the thing, Abby. You seem like a nice girl. And Chase may seem like a nice guy. But..."

"But?"

"I will sound like a nutcase."

"Please tell me."

"Ok. If you know what's good for you, you need to stay away from Chase Jones. Everyone needs to stay away from Chase Jones. Go out with him and you'll only end up getting hurt. Don't let him hurt you, too." Savannah opened the door and stared me dead in the eye. "And don't tell him I said that."

"Promise," I said, crossing my fingers behind my back.

The mystery deepened.

What exactly had Chase Jones done to hurt Savannah?

And why did I feel a twinge of jealousy at the thought of them together?

14

CHASE

*F*all was the best of the four seasons. Football was underway. The mountain air was crisp and the first snowfall would be soon. The trees were already changing colors, morphing into an array of bright yellows, oranges, and reds. I slung my backpack over my shoulder and headed to the Fine Arts Building.

Abby was waiting outside. She had sent me a text saying that she wanted to talk. These days, that kind of text would give me a cold sweat. But since it was Abby, and our relationship was strictly business, I wasn't too concerned.

That changed when I saw the stoic expression on her face.

The cold sweat began.

"What's up?" I asked. She looked pretty with her hair down.

"I have questions." She folded her arms and sized me up with a glare.

What now?

Students passed by. Gone were the t-shirts and skirts of

summer, replaced by the sweaters and jeans of autumn. Not that I was complaining. There was something deliciously cozy about girls in sweaters. Like the white one Abby was wearing.

Whoa, Chase. Stop thinking like that. Strictly business, remember?

"Let's go for a walk," I said. "We could cut through the quad? If we do that, I guarantee people will talk about us like we're a thing."

"Should we hold hands?" Her tone suggested she would rather hold a slug.

"Trust me — we don't need to hold hands. If I stand next to someone long enough, people will think I'm dating them. There was once a rumor I was in a relationship with the school statue." I hoped my joke, unfunny as it was, would put her at ease.

What was with her today, anyway? She had been so funny over the weekend as we texted back and forth, falling into an easy banter with each other.

Abby raised an eyebrow. "Did it dump you after three weeks?"

"We had serious communication issues." I stuck out my arm as a substitute for my hand. "Come on."

She didn't take my arm, but she walked beside me. "So, I spoke with your dancer friend this morning."

Savannah. We'd been broken up for just over a month now, but talking about her still felt like picking open a scab. All at once, a million questions piled into my head, each fighting to reach my mouth. How was she? What did she say? Was she hurt? Was she seeing anyone? Why'd she break up with me?

But all I said was: "Oh."

"We talked about you." Abby eyed me as if I was a test subject in a science lab. Like any good scientist, she was trying to see how I responded. She was testing me. Why? What had Savannah said?

"And did you figure out why she dumped me?"

We circled through the quad. Most of the students left us in peace, busy with their own conversations. But I caught a handful subtly pointing, and at least one took a picture with their cell. Good. The sooner the rumor that Abby and I were an item started, the sooner the saboteur — if there was one — would show their ugly face.

Abby kept her voice low. "She said you hurt her."

"What?" I couldn't keep the surprise out of my voice. Hurt Savannah? How? I'd admit that I wasn't the smoothest talker, wasn't always the best at texting back, but I was sure that I said nothing that could be interpreted as mean. I'd planned all our dates, paid for everything. I didn't push for anything physical — we didn't kiss until our third date, and even then, I kept everything super respectful. How could I have hurt her?

"You didn't know that," Abby said. Her voice was soft, her stoic demeanor melting slightly. "You actually didn't know."

"How could you tell?" I was surprised, again.

"Your face. Your words."

"But I didn't say anything."

"Exactly. If you had hurt her and you knew it, you would deny it. Or you would call her crazy. But you said nothing. And you got the same look on your face you always have when you're thinking hard. It almost looks painful."

"Hey!" I protested, holding my hands up as she laughed at me. "Cheap shot!"

Abby smiled at me and continued. "You looked like you were trying to remember how you could have hurt her. If you don't remember, that means if you did hurt her, it was by accident."

Wow. This girl read me like a book. It's a good thing I

wasn't the type to lie — I wouldn't be able to get away with it even if I wanted to. "I can't think of anything I did."

Abby reached out her hand to me like she was deeming me worthy of an olive branch. Her hand was small, her nails chewed and without polish. I took her hand in mine and smiled at her, glad I was forgiven. And so we were holding hands, in public, at Evermore.

If people were giving us subtle glances before, now they dropped all pretense of subtlety. Some openly gawked.

"Are you sure you're ready for this?" I whispered. "People will talk. And it's not always pretty. Sometimes they're mean."

"Yes, Mr. Quarterback, I have been on the internet before," Abby said. "I once had the mayor's aide show up at my front door and imply that my time at Evermore would be so much nicer if I would just issue a correction on a piece I'd published online."

"And?"

"I told him that his teeth would be so much nicer if he was smart enough to back off."

I almost choked. "You said that?"

Abby paused, grinned. "I wish. I just let him rant for a bit, then closed the door. I left the article up, but the website took it down. A week later they had an exclusive interview with the mayor."

"That's B.S."

"That's journalism," Abby said. She spun so she was facing me, her eyes looking into mine. I immediately missed the warmth of her next to my side. "The point, Chase Jones, is that I don't scare that easy."

Impressive. Who was this girl? Nicholas must've been crazy to not notice her.

"Now. Chase. I need you to think. Even if it's painful." Abby smirked. "There's a chance someone else scared

Savannah off. Do you know anyone who might want to mess with you?"

There was only one name that came to mind: my ex-girlfriend.

Madison Albright.

15

ABBY

*T*he field glowed under the glare of the Friday night lights. In the bleachers, the crowd stomped their feet, clapped their hands, and rang an alarming number of cowbells. My ears already hurt — people enjoyed this? The cheerleaders, dressed in their tiny black outfits emblazoned with silver panthers, waved their pom-poms and danced to the school fight song. Hailey Danielson was at the front of the pack, her caramel ponytail swishing as she moved. She gestured to the rest of her squad, who obediently formed two rows in the corner of the end zone and unfurled a banner.

Chase Jones burst through the banner, tearing it in half. He held his helmet in one hand, the silver striping on his jersey catching the light — number 7, just like his hero, John Elway.

The entire crowd erupted into even louder cheers, and I couldn't help but join in.

It was crazy to think there were already rumors I was dating him. Click hadn't confirmed our relationship, so I was fairly sure the three-week countdown hadn't started. Yet.

Izzy clutched my arm. "I cannot believe you're dating him."

I felt horrible for lying to Izzy about Chase and I, but she had been so overcome with shock when I told her I was hanging out with Chase Jones romantically, that it had been easy to fib for the rest of the conversation. She was too startled to ask tough questions.

Chase looked like an all-star. He played like one too. The game was — as the journalists I'd studied would say — a good, old-fashioned barn burner. Chase carved through the defense like it was a Thanksgiving turkey. But for every successful touchdown pass he threw, the Eastmount Knights answered with a touchdown of their own. It came down to the last play of the game. Evermore was down by four with the ball on the six-yard line.

Chase examined the defense. He stood back. Pointed to one of the defenders. Shouted something to his team. Their formation changed. He was changing the play. Huge murmuring swept the crowded bleachers. I even saw one dad in the front row take off his hat and clutch it to his chest. I momentarily surveyed the dark-haired man: Chase's dad, perhaps?

Chase snapped the ball. Ran to the right. Two of our receivers ran for the end zone, both covered by a pair of defenders. Chase faked the pass, then tucked the ball under his arm and ran for the goal line.

But he would not make it. Two Knight defenders peeled off their receivers and came to meet him. I winced, waiting for him to be tackled to the ground, but at the last second, Chase dove through the air.

All three guys collided with the violence of a car crash, Chase's body spinning. Yet, as he spun, he reached out his arm that held the football. It crossed the goal line as Chase flopped to the ground. He raised a triumphant fist in the air.

Touchdown!

The crowd roared so loudly it felt like the bleachers were about to drop beneath me.

♥

"Good game." I was in the school parking lot, leaning against Chase's Jeep. Izzy had driven me to the game, so Chase could drive me home. It was part of tonight's plan to check a very important mark off my list: Football Party.

Chase smiled. He was freshly showered and dressed in dark jeans and a black t-shirt that somehow made the navy blue of his eyes look even more intense than usual. His hair was the kind of messy that made me want to run my hands through it—

Wait, what? Shut up. Chase was my fake boyfriend. The only hair I wanted to touch belonged to Nicholas.

Didn't it?

I tried to put myself back in business mode, difficult in my party outfit. I was wearing a tight top and the trusty single-pair-of-skinny-jeans-I-owned. I'd borrowed (stolen) the top from Katie, so it was a size too small. Sadly, the tight fit emphasized my chest in a more "lack thereof" than "look at me" way.

I persisted with business Abby nonetheless, narrowing my eyes. "Only took you forty-five minutes to shower and make yourself pretty, Jones, is that a new record? Don't worry, it's not like it's freezing out here or anything."

Chase burst out laughing. "You know you could have waited inside."

I sighed; he was right. And it wasn't freezing, it was positively balmy for October. Chase carried his letterman football jacket balled beneath his arm.

"Turn around. Close your eyes," he said.

I didn't want to stop looking at him.

"Come on, Abs. If you can't trust your fake boyfriend, who can you trust?"

I rolled my eyes and turned away. I felt something warm and heavy wrap around my shoulders. Something that smelled like Chase. His football jacket. So that was how it felt to have a cute boy give you his jacket.

"Thank you."

He opened the passenger door of his Jeep for me. "You gotta look the part. Plus, now you can't complain you're cold anymore."

The victory party was at Hailey Danielson's house. Or should I say, it was at Hailey Danielson's mansion. Hailey was famous at Evermore High for three things:

Adam Zamos, her long-time boyfriend.

Making captain of the cheer squad her junior year.

And having a rich stepdad. Apparently, he was an enormous deal at one of Denver's premier sports agencies. He represented several members of the Broncos and Avalanche.

The mansion had an iron gate — with a silver panther on it, which I assumed would be replaced when Hailey graduated from Evermore — and privacy hedges that were at least ten feet tall. Chase pressed the button on the intercom, told them who he was, and the gate opened smoothly.

"What world am I living in?" I rolled my eyes.

Chase grinned. "The best one. But I'm telling you — you wear that jacket, people will ask some questions." His grin faded. "And Madison's probably here. Maybe it's a bad idea."

I pulled the jacket around me protectively. "Like I said — I don't scare easy."

"We better get our story straight. What are we doing here together?"

"Boyfriend and girlfriend."

Chase waved the thought away. "Can't come out and say

it. Nobody goes straight from a date or two to that label. We haven't even been blasted on Click yet."

Ah, Click. The judge, jury, and executioner of every relationship at Evermore.

"The last person who was officially my girlfriend was Madison. If this was a normal relationship, we'd be trying to hide it a bit, right?" Chase looked at me for my opinion. I nodded, trying to appear like I knew how relationships worked.

"Cool. If anyone asks, say we're hanging out. Let them put it all together," Chase instructed.

I nodded again.

It sounded smart, but it still stung. Just hanging out. It felt so casual. Cheap.

Easy, Abby. It's a fake relationship. And you're only here for your checklist — not to be Chase's date. This is his world, not yours. Focus on getting the material you need.

The doors to Hailey's house swung open.

It was like walking onto a movie set. The entire Evermore elite seemed to be there already. Were we fashionably late?

I recognized a lot of the girls. The cheerleading squad, the beauty queens and yearbook staff, the entire student council roster (why did no guys ever seem to run for student council?), and girls from the soccer and dance teams. Everyone looked painfully glamorous.

The guys were almost all football players, most of them dressed down in Panthers hoodies and t-shirts, their hair still wet from their post-game showers. I wondered why athletes seemed to get so much school branded gear bought for them. Nobody had ever presented me with as much as a single sock for working on the Pinnacle. We didn't even have Evermore-brand stationary.

The party was taking place in Hailey's basement — which had a full wet bar, two pool tables, a piano, and allegedly, a twenty-seat home theater. As we stepped into the room, eyes were on us immediately. It was like we were world famous and had stepped onto the red carpet. I half-expected the flash of a thousand paparazzi cameras.

I could feel the panic rising in me and I instinctively clutched Chase's arm.

"Easy, Abs," he murmured. "They'll get over it. I'll go grab us some drinks. You just do your journalist thing, gather your material or whatever."

He seemed distant now that we were immersed in his world.

Before I could protest — I was definitely not planning on drinking — Chase was gone, and I was hovering near the entrance alone. I watched him stride across the room, fist bumping and high-fiving the guys. I narrowed my eyes as girls lined up to hug him and congratulate him on the team's win.

That was okay, I told myself. I couldn't expect to hang on his arm all night. And at least he had given me an actual reason to be at this party, unlike that last disaster Izzy and I had stumbled through.

The social feature was supposed to be about experiencing high school life at its fullest, not leering at people from behind the star quarterback.

Just have fun.

I grabbed a stool near the pool tables and tried to look casual, tapping my foot to the music. I felt like an imposter.

Payton, the sportswriter for the Pinnacle, sat next to me. She was the only Pinnacle staff member who was classically "popular." Being the football coach's daughter gave her an automatic pass in a place like Evermore. She only ever covered sports.

"So, you and Chase, huh?" she said perkily. "Who would

have thought it? The all-star quarterback with a lowly journalist. Good for you!"

"It's nothing," I replied.

"You're wearing his jacket."

"I was cold."

"Suuuuuuure." Payton stared at Chase the way a cat stared at a mouse. She did everything but lick her lips. "I heard he's a great kisser. Is it true?"

I'd never felt so uncomfortable in my life.

I wouldn't know, I've never kissed him. And even if I had kissed him, it's not like I had a point of reference.

My face flared red as I searched for an answer that was anything but the mortifying truth, which I obviously couldn't say out loud.

Just when I didn't think my discomfort could grow, Madison Albright, Chase's ex-girlfriend, took a seat on the stool next to me.

Great. I was surrounded. Chase was pouring drinks at the bar, chatting to Dylan Ramirez and a couple of other guys from the team.

Madison had never even looked at me in her life before tonight, but here we were. "Abby, Payton!" she squealed like we were long lost best friends. Madison wore her self-assurance like a weapon, brimming confidence and poise. Even when you knew all the rumors, being near that much charisma was intoxicating. No wonder Chase had fallen for her.

In fact, the only boy who had ever rejected her advances was Trey Carter, Evermore's resident bad boy. Girls would line up around city blocks for a chance to date Trey — if they weren't scared of him. According to Click, after her breakup with Chase, Madison went after Trey. He laughed in her face. It was probably the only time a boy had ever humbled Madison. I didn't know if it was true or not, but it made me happy to think about.

"Chase's jacket looks great on you," Madison said, way too enthusiastically. "It fits perfectly. It was always too big on me. But on you it just looks so cozy. Like you were born to wear it."

"Thanks?" I wasn't stupid. I knew she was insulting me. And I knew her statement wasn't true — the jacket was huge on me. Unfortunately, I did not have a clever comeback. All I could do was scan the room for Chase, hoping he would be back soon. Now he was at the bar with two drinks in his hand, talking to one of the younger players. It looked like Chase was trying to cheer the other guy up.

There he goes, being a good person just when I need him, I thought bitterly.

"Have you kissed yet?" Madison asked. I looked up at her, completely trapped. Madison was one of those girls who lived to make people uncomfortable. I now knew how a fly felt when it was caught in a spider web.

Payton hid her smirk.

"It's okay," Madison said. "I won't tell. He's an amazing kisser, right?"

I had to say something. Anything. "Sure?"

Madison's perfectly groomed eyebrows shot up. "Oh, so you have kissed him."

Every question was a landmine, and I'd already lost both my legs. This was how it felt to be on the other end of one of my interrogation attempts. I tried to tell myself this was good practice for journalistic empathy. "I didn't say that."

"So, have you?" Madison fluttered her eyelashes like she was straight out of a Disney movie.

"Have you?" I shot back. Oof, wrong question Abby, you dummy.

Madison grinned evilly. "I think you know the answer to that."

She put her arm around me and pulled me so I almost fell off my stool. She put her lips near my ear. Her perfume was over-powering. I felt nauseous. "I've seen you, running around after him like a lost puppy. You might think it's cute, but it's pathetic. Everyone thinks it is. And if you're hoping that you can be his little drunken mistake tonight, I have some bad news for you. Chase Jones doesn't make mistakes, and he doesn't drink. So you're probably out of the running. Enjoy his jacket though."

And with that, Madison was off to sink her claws into someone else.

Payton looked as shocked as I felt.

"What a b—"

"How're my two favorite hard-hitting journalists?" Chase returned — finally — cutting Payton off. Which was a shame, because I was about to fully agree with her sentiment.

Payton laughed and took one of the red cups Chase was holding. I was pretty sure it was for me, but Payton either didn't notice or didn't care, and Chase didn't protest. She bantered with Chase for a moment while I simmered, drinkless.

As far as I was concerned, Madison Albright was behind everything wrong with the world.

"Abs. Anyone home?" Chase placed his drink in my hand and jokingly waved in front of my face. "You look like you're about to boil over. Take a sip. Relax."

Payton had left, pulled away by Hailey.

I looked down at the fizzy brown drink in the cup.

"It's fine. I don't really drink."

"It's Pepsi," Chase said. "And you look like you could use something that'll cool you down."

Oh. Pepsi.

"Sorry, it's… just a rule my dad has. If you're at a party, don't take a drink that's not sealed, or you didn't make yourself."

Chase took the drink back. "My bad, I didn't even think of — I'll grab you a can. What do you want?"

"Ginger ale?"

He smiled. "Back in a flash."

And he was, this time — with a can of Ginger Ale. It hissed as I opened it, and I drank a mouthful.

Just then, a bundle of energy came running up to us. "What's up, party people?"

She elbowed Chase in the ribs. "Hey all-star, introduce me!"

The girl's navy eyes sparkled. Jordyn Jones, Chase's twin sister. She was a shorter, fairer version of Chase — the resemblance was uncanny.

"I guess they let anyone into these parties now, huh?" Chase teased. "This is Jordyn. My younger twin sister."

"Younger?"

"By seven minutes," Chase said. "And this is my friend, Abby. She's a bit weird."

"The best ones usually are," Jordyn said. She stuck out her hand. "I just wanted to thank you."

"Thank me?" Color me confused.

"Normally this one's a bit of a grump," Jordyn said. "But he's been in a good mood lately. Between you and me, I think you're the reason why."

My eyes bugged at her comment.

Chase grabbed his sister and redirected her. "Hailey's calling you."

"I'm going, I'm going." Jordyn flashed a peace sign. "Later. Don't do anything I would do."

After she was gone, I glanced at Chase. "Friend?"

"I don't lie to Jordyn," he said flatly. "Non-negotiable. But

I can't tell her the whole truth. So, I'm just going to let her think what she wants and not correct her."

Fair enough.

"Did you tell anyone about us?" I asked, choosing my words cautiously.

"No. You?"

"No." I hadn't even told Izzy the truth.

Wanting to change the subject, I eyed the cup of Pepsi he was now sipping. "You don't drink?"

"Couldn't even if I wanted to," he said.

"Because it's football season?"

"Yeah, partly. I need to stay focused."

"Because you're driving me home?"

"That too." He stood next to me and gestured to the party. "What do you see?"

"Teenagers getting ready to make stupid decisions."

"And what does every teenager have?"

"A bad attitude."

"No, that's just you." He grinned down at me.

I tried to glare at him, but my smile betrayed me.

"They have phones," he said. "Cameras. I drink, get caught, maybe the coach has some words for me. I get drunk, do something stupid and it goes viral on Click? Kicked off the team. Scholarship opportunities? Gone."

"Like any high school will get rid of their starting quarterback."

"Coach Clarence would," Chase replied. "He takes stuff like this seriously."

"So, what about them?" I gestured to a cluster of players across the room.

"That's why I wanted to read the article before you submitted it," he said. "Can't have you naming names and ruining lives, Abigail Murrow. But there are other reasons, too."

Even though Chase seemed like he was different from the rest of the football guys, I'd assumed that deep down he was the same. He wanted to get drunk, play football, and break a few hearts on his way to a full scholarship. I'd expected that side of Chase to be on full display at a victory party. But, if anything, he was more reserved than I'd ever seen him. I felt bad for my earlier catty thoughts about the girls he was talking to.

"Every summer Evermore runs a training camp for kids who want to play football. I've helped coach at it every year since the start of high school. I know those kids, they know me. If they see pictures and videos of me getting trashed, what are they going to think?"

I looked up at this impossibly good-looking star quarter-back, at a high school party with all of his friends, but standing with me in the corner, telling me things that were causing me to like him way more than I would have ever imagined.

Strictly business, I reminded myself. This relationship needed to stay strictly business. Anyway, standing with me at the party was part of the plan to catch the saboteur. Once we had figured out who was sabotaging Chase Jones, our pact, and probably friendship — if you could call it that — would be over.

While my brain got the idea, my heart wasn't receiving the message.

16

ABBY

One public appearance wearing Chase Jones' football jacket and rumors flew. Some people said we were dating. They said it was serious. One rumor claimed that Chase had already given me a promise ring. I can't deny that rumor made me feel smug for a few seconds.

But then other people had responded to these posts — anonymously, of course — saying that I was just following Chase around because I was writing a social feature for the Pinnacle. Others demanded to know my identity. They'd never seen this girl before. Who was she? A transfer student or something? They often followed up these comments with something like — a guy like Chase Jones wouldn't be caught dead with a girl like her. A nobody.

Ouch.

I didn't scare easily, but I still had feelings.

On Sunday morning, I shoved those feelings aside to get back to work on uncovering the problems with Chase's previous relationships. I scrambled to find a decent outfit for my excursion, and I made a mental note to go shopping soon. Izzy would love an excuse for a girls' shopping trip.

Sunday mornings on Main Street were a cacophony of chaos. It was the last weekend the Farmers' Market would be open before shutting down for the winter. Hundreds of stalls sat in the middle of the brick path. Jewelry dangled from hooks and caught the morning sun. Girls approached with perfume bottles, and if you weren't quick, they'd spray it on you and launch into a spiel about how it was made from 100% organically grown coconut oil and sustainably sourced vanilla. I did my best to avoid eye contact with, well, everyone.

On the far end of Main Street I found the place I was looking for: Red Rainbow Diner. A bright blue awning hung over the entry and the store window was painted with — you guessed it — a red rainbow. Inside, historic photos of the town hung from the light blue walls. Red Rainbow Diner was straight vintage, designed to look exactly like a diner from the 1950s. It was also the place to go for brunch on a weekend.

The smell of sizzling bacon and strong coffee washed over me. My stomach grumbled. Sadly, I wasn't here to indulge. I had another purpose.

Savannah sat in a booth in the back corner, surrounded by other dancers. I'd discreetly started following the dance troupe's social media account — using an anonymous account of my own — so I could monitor Savannah's social life. And, more importantly, so I could stage accidental-on-purpose run-ins.

It didn't take her long to notice me.

I pretended to look at the selection of freshly baked cinnamon buns as she waltzed over.

"I wish they didn't have raisins," she said. "I hate raisins."

I felt a pang of sympathy. Her conversational openers were almost as bad as mine. "Me too. How are you?"

"Good," she said.

I waited. As Chase's most recent ex, there was no way she had not heard the news that he might be dating me — even if we weren't official by Click's standards.

"Are you waiting for someone?" she asked.

"Just grabbing and going," I said. I grabbed two cinnamon buns. The second one was actually for Izzy, but I let Savannah draw her own assumptions.

"So, you and Chase?"

I shrugged, non-committal. "We're just hanging out."

"You should… never mind."

My interest was piqued. "What?"

"It's not important."

"Tell me."

Savannah tossed her red hair back. She looked around to make sure no one was paying attention to us. They weren't — everyone was too busy shoving delicious food into their mouths. "Look… I'm only telling this because you seem nice. Innocent."

I narrowed my eyes at her word choice, even though I realized she didn't mean it as an insult. She seemed like a genuinely kind person. "You need to be careful with Chase."

"He seems harmless to me." I counted out change for my cinnamon buns and waited for her to elaborate.

"He's not what he seems like." She insisted, crossing her arms.

"Okay." I said.

"It's just…"

Yes! She would talk. It was time to go in for the kill.

I gave her a friendly smile. "I appreciate what you're trying to do. I do. But you can't just say things. Give me something I can go off of. What did he do that was so bad?"

"He cheated."

WHAT? I fumbled with my cinnamon buns and they fell to the floor. I quickly picked them up, grateful that they were covered in plastic wrap. Chase Jones CHEATED? That seemed so unlike the boy I was starting to know. Even though we were only in a fake relationship I hadn't seen him flirt with any other girls. Talk to them — yes. Many of them, in fact. But he always seemed so kind, so genuine.

"Are you sure?" There was a slight tremble in my voice.

"Yes. Look, we never did the official boyfriend-girlfriend label or anything, but after we were dating for about two weeks, he told me he didn't want to see anyone else. That he liked me, liked where it was going. He said he wouldn't see anyone else and asked me if I wouldn't either."

She stopped suddenly, looking aghast, like she'd said too much.

"I won't tell anyone."

"Promise?" she asked. "This is strictly off the record."

"I know." I smiled. I would never pull this nice girl through the mud for a story. "So how did you find out? Did he confess or something?"

"Someone sent me a picture on Click."

Through Click, you could anonymously send photos to other users with short captions. Best of all, the photos disappeared in ten seconds and you couldn't take a screenshot. It was the perfect way to start fires without getting burnt. So typically Evermore.

"A picture of…?"

"Chase. Kissing another girl." Savannah lowered her voice. "I got it on the first day of school. It came through with a caption. Look what you missed last week." She sighed. "We'd only been going out for a couple weeks. But he'd promised — no one else. Then I see that? It hurt. So, I broke up with him."

"I'm so sorry," I said. "I didn't know."

"No one does. I don't even think he knows that I saw it." She smiled. "Just… be careful, okay? Sometimes the sweetest boys are the most dangerous."

Sometimes they were indeed.

CHASE

*A*bby's replies to my texts throughout the week were short, and when I asked her if she wanted to do something, she always seemed busy. On the weekend, she didn't text me at all. I tried not to think about it too much. She wasn't much of a texter — she said she preferred to talk face to face. You couldn't account for tone or body language over a text.

By Monday morning, I hadn't received a single text since last Friday, when she wished me luck before a game. That had me concerned. And, if I'm being honest, a little disappointed.

Strictly business, Chase, I reminded myself, and so I didn't text her either.

I was growing fond of Abby. I liked having her around. Would she want to be friends with me when all of this was over? Probably not. She seemed so removed from school and all of its activities, like she was above it all. How would we stay friends when our worlds would never collide again?

The prospect bothered me. And it bothered me that it bothered me.

The teacher finished drawing out a math equation on the whiteboard as the bell rang. Before we left, she reminded us we would have a quiz on quadrilateral equations at the end of the week. Fun. I'd have to find time after practice to cram with Dylan. When he wasn't bowling over linebackers, he was killing it in math class. Dylan, unlike me, didn't have too much trouble keeping his grades up during football season. I teetered on the line constantly, barely maintaining the C average I needed to keep playing every Friday night. Sometimes I wondered if teachers gave me C's when I didn't even earn them.

As promised in her last text on Friday, Abby was waiting for me outside of math class. Her expression was impassive as usual, her green eyes searching my every movement for... something. That was one thing that made Abby different from other girls I dated. I could never tell what she was thinking.

"How was your weekend, fake girlfriend?" I asked, keeping my voice low. I smiled at her, hoping she would do the same back.

She didn't. "It was interesting."

"Something you need to talk about?"

"Not here."

We walked to the quad in relative silence. I tried to drag something out of her, but she only gifted me with one-word answers. We found a bench that was relatively secluded and sat.

Abby faced me and immediately dropped a bomb. "You need to tell me the truth, Chase Jones. Did you cheat on Savannah?"

Did I WHAT?

I must have looked completely appalled, because for the first time that day, a ghost of a smile appeared on her lips.

"I will swear on my life that I did not." I looked her dead in the eye.

"You're not lying to me, are you?"

Never. Even if I wanted to lie to her, I couldn't. "I promise. Cross my heart, hope to die."

Finally, she gave me a full, sincere smile.

It was almost too bright and too comforting. I had to look away before I blushed. "I swear. We weren't official, but I told her I didn't want to see anyone else. And I didn't."

"I believe you." Abby's smile faded and her professional demeanor returned. "Unfortunately, Savannah thinks otherwise."

Now I was completely confused.

"The day Savannah broke up with you, someone sent her a picture through Click. It was of you and another girl, and you were kissing. Savannah said the same as you, that you weren't like official or anything, but…"

If I liked a girl and saw a photo of her with another dude, I'd be choked. Savannah was sensitive, too. It must have hurt her bad. I wanted to say something to her, to apologize for getting her involved in my crazy life, but somehow, I thought that would make things worse. "Did she show you the picture?"

"Click deletes pictures."

That stupid app.

"She said it was with you and a girl she didn't recognize. It was from behind, and the caption said it was from the week before. You could only see the back of her head, but your face was turned towards her. You were on Main Street."

Wait. Main Street? The week before she dumped me?

"It wasn't me," I said.

Abby looked at me curiously. "How do you know?"

"I wasn't in town."

"Where were you?"

"Colorado State runs a summer camp for players all over the state right before school starts back. I go every year. I was staying in the dorms with a bunch of other dudes. And they supervised us hard. Strict curfews or they kicked you out of camp. Something to do with NCAA regulations, probably."

"Interesting." Abby grinned in the cute way she always did when she was unravelling something in her mind. "Well, Mr. Quarterback, I think we can safely say that someone is definitely trying to sabotage your relationships."

"Madison," I said immediately.

"She's the most likely culprit, but we don't have any hard evidence. And if you don't have any evidence, Savannah will not believe you. And she's definitely not going to give you another shot."

Why would I want another shot at Savannah?

Oh.

Right.

I was supposed to still have a crush on her and not be developing —

No, Chase. Strictly. Business.

"So, what's our next move?" I asked. I figured I'd let her take the lead. The more time I spent with Abby, the more intelligent I realized she was. Smarter than me for sure.

"To go to the cafeteria."

I couldn't quite connect the dots, but I trusted her lead. We crossed the quad and arrived at Evermore's main building, which housed most of the regular classes and the cafeteria. We stood at the entrance to the cafeteria.

"Are you ready?" she asked, a mischievous grin on her face.

"Ready for what?"

"To be my official fake boyfriend." She grabbed my hand and practically pulled it around her shoulder.

A light went on in my brain.

"Let's do this." We stepped into the cafeteria, and I tightened my grip around her. She fit perfectly under my arm. Abby nuzzled into my chest as we walked. My heart skipped a beat at her closeness, before I shook myself off and remembered she was acting. Remembered we were acting.

And so I played the part. If anyone had doubts about us being together before, this would squish all of them dead. I dropped a kiss on the top of her head. Her hair smelled like coconuts.

She looked up at me, flushed. Oops, maybe too far.

I tried to silently communicate "sorry" with my eyes, but she was stepping away from me.

She took both my hands and squeezed them. Man, she was good at this acting stuff.

"I'll see you later," she said. For a moment, it looked like she would kiss my cheek. But at the last second, she backed away and instead brushed off my jacket and adjusted my collar. Her cheeks were pink.

"Bye," I replied, and I stood there, still for a moment, watching her as she walked away.

Abigail Murrow, I hope you're as brave as you say you are, because I'm sure you just started the three-week countdown.

ABBY

*D*on't tell anyone, but I'd never, ever been on a date before. Dates were something that happened to other people. It's not like I hadn't thought about what a date would be like though.

I imagined a cute boy picking me up and taking me to a burger joint, where we'd split a chocolate milkshake — which I would regret because I wanted a whole milkshake to myself. He'd make small talk as he dropped me off, and then he'd walk me to my door. We would stand there, sort of awkwardly, as he stumbled over his words trying to figure out whether to kiss me. Eventually, he would, and it would be perfect.

Nowhere in my fantasies did I imagine that the date would start with me wanting to throw up.

I paced a hole in the floor of my bedroom, my stomach flipping like a carnival ride.

What was wrong with me? I should be calm and collected. I'd spent the entire day preparing. First, Izzy and I had gone shopping and spent some long overdue girl time together. With Izzy's help, I found the perfect date outfit for the cool,

October weather: a deep grey sweater dress, tights and black ankle boots. Next, I went home, washed my hair, and roped Katie into curling it for me. She grudgingly obliged after I promised to do her laundry for the next month. It ended up being fun styling hair with my little sister.

I tried out my new mascara wand, careful not to stab myself in the eye, and added lip gloss. Cherry Kiss — as if I would kiss anyone on a fake date.

How did girls do all of this every morning before school? It was so much work!

I sent a picture of my finished look to Izzy, and she sent a smiley face and a thumbs up back. Izzy's highest form of approval.

And then I almost texted Chase to call the entire thing off.

Why was I so nervous?

WHY?

This was a fake date.

With a fake boyfriend.

That I had insisted on. My idea, not his.

Apparently, it was also a marvelous time for an anxiety attack. I practiced taking deep breaths through my nose, then exhaling through my mouth. It calmed me down a little, but my hands were still trembling.

"Knock knock." My dad stood at my bedroom door.

"Instead of saying knock knock, you could always, you know, knock." I paced and tried to push every thought from my mind. What if I said something stupid to Chase? What if I embarrassed myself? Like if I laughed and food came out of my nose? Or even worse… What if I embarrassed HIM? What if, what if, what if?

"You look wonderful. What's the boy's name again?"

"Chase," I mumbled.

"What happened to Chase being just a friend?"

"He is just a friend." I insisted.

Well, fake boyfriend to be exact, but I would hardly explain that one to my father.

Tonight was just practice for the real thing; a lesson in clichés. So why was I so nervous?

"How do you feel?" Dad asked.

"Nervous."

"Good. You're supposed to be nervous."

"Really? Because when I picture the perfect high school date in my head, I'm effortlessly cool."

Dad laughed. "You're my daughter, and I love you more than anything, but not once in your life have you been effortlessly cool."

"Thanks for the pep talk, Dad."

"Come here." Dad gave me a reassuring hug. "You don't have to be perfect. You just have to be yourself."

"Such a cliché."

"Clichés are popular for a reason," Dad said. "Just have fun. Don't take everything so seriously. What's the worst that could happen?"

"Public humiliation."

Dad sat on the end of my bed while I paced. "You can get through public humiliation. Want to know how I know?"

Yes.

"I was seven," Dad said. "I was at summer camp. My eighth birthday was at the end of the week. There was a girl — Heather — and I had a crush on her. She was eight. And somehow, I knew — I KNEW — that for a girl to like a boy, the boy had to be older than her."

I stopped pacing. "That is a statistical fact. You were a wise seven-year-old."

"Not that wise," Dad said. "When Heather asked how old I was, I said I was nine. One year older than her."

I stifled a laugh. "You lied about your age when you were seven?"

"I liked her," Dad said, shrugging. "So, it's the end of the week. Heather is sitting at my table with her parents. To my surprise, they bring out a birthday cake. And they make me stand on a chair while they sing to me. But there's a problem — the birthday cake only has eight candles."

"Oh no…"

"And Heather — sharp as she was — points this out. She interrupts my happy birthday song. 'The cake is wrong; it only has eight candles. It should have ten. Why doesn't have ten?' My parents burst out laughing. And I have to sit there while they explain to Heather that I'm actually seven turning eight, not nine turning ten, like I said."

I couldn't help it — I laughed. I pictured my dad, cheeks rosy, lips pressed together furiously. An angry actually-eight-year-old with his plan foiled by well-meaning adults. "What did you do?" I asked between fits of laughter. "How did you explain it?"

"I didn't. I crawled under the table and stayed there until dinner was over."

"Oh, Dad."

"I know." He smiled, chuckling at himself. "The point is, we're tough, us Murrows. We can survive anything."

Somehow, my nerves had disappeared. "Thanks, Dad. For everything."

Then the doorbell rang.

My nerves crashed down on me.

Dad stood and cleared his throat. He shot me a devilish smile. "Time to be Mr. Overprotective."

19

CHASE

I stood a respectful distance from the front step. Prior to the date, an argument raged in my head: is it more cliché to bring flowers or chocolates to a first date? I knew Abby wanted the perfect cliché first date. I eventually settled on a dozen chocolate flowers... though I'd eaten half of them during the planning phase.

Abby's father opened the door, I could tell who he was immediately. He had the same green eyes as Abby, the same stoic expression.

"I'm Mr. Murrow," he said seriously.

We shook hands. "Chase Jones. I'm here for—"

"I know why you're here," he said, still gripping my hand, hard. "You're trying to get my daughter pregnant."

I stared at the man in complete disbelief for a second, openmouthed. Did I hear him wrong? Before I could respond — not that I could think of anything to say — he burst out laughing.

"I've always wanted to do that. Sorry, I couldn't help myself!" His serious demeanor disappeared, the stoic look replaced with a smile you'd imagine on a young Santa Claus.

He was still chuckling to himself when he opened the door wider.

"Don't mind my lunatic father." Abby was standing behind the door, glowering at her dad. She whirled to face me, her gaze moving from her still-laughing father.

We stared at each other and my mind went totally blank. Abby. Looked. Hot.

She must have taken my surprise for something else. She smoothed her dress. "Is it okay?"

"It's great!" I reassured quickly, glad to finally have two coherent words to say. I gave her the half-dozen chocolate roses.

She pretended to smell them. "Beautiful, two clichés in one. Dad, can you find a vase for these?"

He took the roses from her. "I'll cut the stems, but I can't promise Katie won't eat them. You two kids have fun. And remember — teen pregnancy is a veritable epidemic."

"Thanks again, Dad," Abby said sarcastically. She closed the door. "So sorry you had to meet him."

"Weirdness runs in the family, huh?"

She shoved me playfully.

I extended my arm and winked. "It's all part of the first date experience."

"I'll mark it off on my checklist — have your dad embarrass you."

"And threaten your date." I raised my eyebrows. Now I knew exactly where Abby got her sarcastic wit from. Meeting her father — even briefly — gave me a glimpse into a whole new side of Abby's life. One that I longed to see more of.

"He's a teddy bear," she said.

I opened the passenger door. "And so begins your perfect cliché date."

20

ABBY

*C*hase had outdone himself. He had turned up with the perfect combination of chocolates and flowers. He wore a navy-blue shirt, dark pants, and an expensive-looking jacket. I'd never seen him dressed up before, and somehow, I was acutely aware that he looked even more handsome than usual. I felt my heartbeat in my throat.

On the drive, he put on a Spotify playlist of the cheesiest love songs he could find.

"The best musical clichés you can imagine, all the sappiest love songs, especially for you." He drummed his fingers on the steering wheel and sung a quick lyric off-key. At least there was one thing Chase wasn't good at. "Jordyn helped me make it. I told her you were a sucker for terrible cheesy music."

I half-laughed, half-groaned, "Oh great, now your sister will think I have the worst taste!"

Chase laughed. "Whatever. She likes you."

"Who, Jordyn?" A pleasant glow settled over me at the thought. Chase's sister was popular and universally well-liked at Evermore.

"I believe her exact words were: it's about time you dated someone smarter than a lamppost. You have a sister too, right?"

"Katie. She would be the gremlin responsible for my lovely hair tonight."

"My compliments to the stylist." We pulled up to a stoplight. "Your mom must love having girls. Mine always says that having me and Jordyn was like having two boys. Jordie was obsessed with playing soccer and trading Pokémon with Dylan and I. She still is deep into all of that geek stuff; she's just gotten better at hiding it."

Ah, family drama. I always knew it would come back to bite me. "Mom's… she's not really around right now. Like we have our phone calls, but I haven't seen her since summer. It's basically me, Katie, and Dad." I hoped I didn't sound as awkward as I felt.

"Sorry, didn't know."

"It's okay," I said. "Honestly, they're both better off this way."

We drove in silence while the theme from Titanic finished. I decided to change the conversation. "Any more thoughts about Madison sabotaging you?"

"Nope," Chase said quickly. "You're not allowed."

"Allowed what?"

"To talk business on a fake date. Rule number one for dating: never talk about your exes. Even on a fake date."

"Right." That's what this was, wasn't it? Fake? I needed to keep that in mind. Sometimes I worried I was losing track of what was real and what wasn't with Chase and I. Were we friends now, underneath this facade? Or was even that part fake? The thought hurt to think about.

We parked near the river that cut through the center of town. He offered me his jacket, which I took — because it was part of the cliché first date. I pulled it tight around my shoulders, enjoying the faint scent of Chase's cologne. He took my hand and guided me down a set of steep stairs to a wooden pathway that hugged the bank of the river.

Chase cleared his throat. "May I present you with: the Riverwalk. The ideal cliché first date location."

The Riverwalk was an arching wooden pathway that ran alongside the river for about three miles. It was lit with string lights, and restaurants and cafes lined both sides of the pedestrian walk. Some eateries had patios that extended out into the river, glowing with heat lamps. The whole place was always crowded with pedestrians, and at the fancier restaurants, it was nearly impossible to get a table unless you booked decades in advance.

Or you knew the right people.

Had Chase got a table at a fancy restaurant? Like one where you were supposed to know which fork to use with which course? I had a moment of panic. "Where are you taking me?"

"For dinner."

"Where?"

He winked. "You'll see."

We walked along the path and made idle conversation. Everything was perfect. Part of me bathed in the magic that was my first date. But the other part of me? It was weighed down by the reality that all of these firsts didn't count. This date was not real.

The river lapped against the wooden platforms as we walked and walked. We passed restaurants with food I didn't even know how to eat, never mind pronounce. A waiter cut in front of us. He was holding a plate with snails fried in garlic butter.

"Please tell me we're not eating here," I said, just loud enough for the waiter to shoot me a dirty look.

Chase snickered. "Don't worry. I've found us a much

better place. They only serve free-range organic snails."

My entire body relaxed at his joke.

"Suddenly I'm no longer hungry." I retorted with a grin.

"That's too bad, because I think you will love the place I'm taking you."

It dawned on me that I would miss Chase when this was over.

We reached the end of the Riverwalk, but we hadn't stopped at a restaurant.

Had we missed it?

Chase checked to make sure no one was looking, then climbed over the wooden fence and onto the sandy river embankment. "Come on, just a bit further."

Where exactly were we going? "What happened to the clichés, Jones? There is nothing cliché about climbing over a fence while I'm all dressed up."

Chase laughed and held out his hand to help me as I clambered over the fence — which was surprisingly difficult to do in a dress.

I fixed him with a mock-glare. "You better not push me in the river."

"I promise," he said. "And that goes for you, too."

I looked at him seriously. "I can't make that promise."

"I guess I'll watch my back."

"You should."

My shoes sunk into the sand, and the Riverwalk faded behind us. It was getting darker now, the first stars appearing in the night sky. Just when I was sure Chase was playing an elaborate practical joke and was leading me nowhere, we rounded a bend and found a handful of square tables set out on a flat beach area by the river. Each table had a checkered red and white tablecloth draped over top. Three were occupied — other couples on dates, it looked like — and one was empty.

Chase took me to the empty table and pulled out my chair.

"What is this?" I asked, taken aback.

As he sat, a waiter arrived to provide an answer.

It was Dylan Ramirez, Chase's best friend. He wore an apron that had 'Beachbreak Burgers' splashed across the front in a loud blue font.

"Welcome to Beachbreak." Dylan grinned.

Beachbreak Burgers was a small, family-run burger joint famous for their amazing burgers and shakes. I went there plenty, but this was all new to me.

The main restaurant — where 99% of people ate — was located at the top of the river. Dylan explained that at the back there was a hidden staircase that led to the beach area, and that they kept it top secret. It was by reservation only. They kept it as secret as possible — if you wanted the beach experience, you had to know someone.

I couldn't believe it. Yet another taste of a life I had never been part of. I imagined Chase, Dylan and their friends bringing girls from the cheerleading team here.

Dylan took our order and gave me a grin. "This had better not end up in the Pinnacle!"

"Please, I would never want something like this to leak. You'll never let me come back then."

Dylan walked away laughing.

I couldn't contain my smile. "This is not at all the cliché first date."

Chase grinned. "Technically — burgers and fries on the Riverwalk? That is totally the cliché first date. I just added a little twist."

Little twist? This was hardly a little twist. This was like walking from real life into a Hallmark movie. An extra cheesy one.

He gave me a strange look. "Is it ok? Would you have

preferred something more straightforward, an average cliché? Like Romano's or something?" He named the romantic Italian restaurant on Main Street that was always full of couples glowing at each other over the candlelight.

"Well you have created a problem."

He raised his eyebrows.

"How are any actual boyfriends going to measure up to my fake boyfriend?"

"They're not. It's a common problem after you date me."

I playfully swatted him, then smiled. "It's perfect. But I have to know. Do you take all the girls here?"

There was no way — NO WAY — he conjured this miracle just for me.

"Can I tell you a secret?"

"I think we're past you needing to ask that question." I laughed nonchalantly, but I felt my heart beating faster.

"Well, to break my own rule about talking about exes, I took Madison here, once. It was the only time I took anyone here. She hated it. Wouldn't even sit at the table. Said there wasn't enough light for her to get a good picture for Click. We left and went to Romano's." Chase smiled wryly at the memory.

Madison, I decided, was an idiot.

"You and Madison... I don't know her well or anything... but you guys don't seem..."

"You mean you can't work out how we dated for almost a year?" Chase laughed, cutting me off.

"Yeah." I said. "You're nice. She has the personality of sour milk."

Chase sighed. "She's complicated. Loves her social media, but only because she's insecure. At first, when we were alone, she was nice. Really nice. But, ultimately, she liked the idea of me more than she liked actual me. Would she have gone out with me if I wasn't the starting quarterback? The question got louder and louder the longer we dated. And at one point, I realized the answer was no. So, I asked her. She deflected and told me to not quit the football team. Made it pretty obvious, so I ended it. Still hurt, though. She was my only serious relationship."

I sat quietly as Chase talked. I always thought everything was so perfect for him, so easy. I never considered that he would struggle with insecurities like any other teenager, but just differently. People used him for his status.

I suddenly felt grateful for my relative invisibility. "I'm sorry."

"Hey, it's cool. I'm over it. She's a nice girl, deep down. Like really deep."

"So how do you do it?" I asked. "How do you trust anyone when everyone could be using you?"

"I don't," he said with a casual shrug. "Not really. Dylan, Jordyn. Trust them both with my life. They're always honest — sometimes painfully honest — but they've always got my back."

Chase paused and locked his eyes on mine.

A shiver flew down my spine.

"And you, Abby," he said. "You've got the same painful honesty."

My heart lurched and guilt surged through me. He trusted me, but I hadn't told him the whole truth.

Dylan returned with our food and I pushed the thought aside, concentrating on my fries.

"Ready for cliché date, part two?" Chase asked after we finished. "It's even better than part one."

That was impossible. But as I was quickly finding out, the impossible became very possible when you spent time with Chase Jones.

ABBY

"I thought we agreed on dinner and a movie?" I said.

"We did." Chase smiled.

"Then why are we in the middle of nowhere?"

"For the movie."

I was confused. After leaving Beachbreak Burgers, we hopped in Chase's Jeep. I assumed he would drive us to the movie theater. Instead, he pulled onto the freeway and drove until the city lights faded. Every time I asked where we were going, he gave the same answer. To the movie.

One bumpy dirt road and a million unanswered questions later, we parked in an empty field. Chase killed the engine. A salt sprinkle of stars danced across the night sky.

"Is this where you murder me, Jones?"

Chase shot me a wicked grin. "Exactly." He handed me a grocery bag from the back of the Jeep. "Snacks for the occasion."

I peered inside the bag to find two giant bags of kettle corn. My favorite.

He remembered.

"And if you'll excuse me for a minute..." Chase disappeared behind the Jeep and opened the tailgate.

What did he have planned? I tore into a bag of kettle corn, the sweet and salty mix swirling on my tongue. My heart was jumping in my chest. Here I was, alone, in the middle of nowhere with Chase Jones.

Chase Jones, who was making my heart beat way too fast.

What was he doing? And why did we come out into the middle of nowhere? Maybe he would pull out a telescope and we would look at the stars together. No, that would be more of a Nicholas move.

Nicholas. I hadn't thought about him in forever. Why not? Wasn't one of my main motivations for this fake relationship to get Nicholas's attention? I LIKED Nicholas.

Didn't I?

I decided not to let my thoughts follow those train tracks. They were bound to derail everything. This was my first date, even if it was fake. I was supposed to enjoy it, not fret.

Chase appeared at the passenger side of the Jeep and opened the door for me. "May I escort you to your seat, my lady?"

Under the moonlight, he was even hotter than usual. I had a sudden, crazy urge to jump into his arms as I climbed out of the vehicle.

Stop it, Abby! This is a fake date! He is doing you a favor; it means NOTHING. You like Nicholas, Chase likes Savannah. You've just become good friends. Buds. Pals. That's all.

Chase preened, a proud peacock. I wondered if whatever was going on was something he had done in the past for real with anyone. Savannah? Madison?

Was I jealous? I shoved the thought aside.

"Hey, Mr. Quarterback, what cliché is this one?" I tried to make my voice sound normal to disguise my pounding heart.

"You'll see." Chase put his hands over my eyes and gently led me a few steps. "Welcome to the Jones Family Drive-in Movie Theater." He pulled his hands away.

No. Freaking. Way.

This was not happening.

ABBY

*L*anterns dotted the area surrounding the Jeep, illuminating the darkness like fireflies. Ahead of us, a white sheet was pulled tight between two trees with lengths of rope.

The tailgate was littered with a stack of blankets and pillows, and a laptop lay in the middle.

"I've reserved the best seat in the house," Chase said.

Still speechless, I climbed into the trunk and leaned back against a pillow. Whoa.

Chase climbed in and sat down next to me, close enough for our shoulders to touch. He flipped open his laptop and plugged a tiny projector into the USB slot. A black-and-white image appeared on the sheet.

Chase turned around to grin at me, excited. "Tonight, we will be playing a back to back of the finest vintage B-Movie horror classics I could conjure: Killer Klowns from Outer Space and, of course, The Blob. Only the best for the lady."

Was this actually happening?

Chase grinned at me again. "But seriously, I hate horror movies, so you might need to hold my hand."

CHASE

I held my smile as long as I could. I don't know what I expected. Applause? An approving nod? A declaration of love? I couldn't read Abby's expression. There was definite shock and surprise, but I couldn't tell if it was the good kind or the bad kind. Did I go too far in my attempt to make her first date memorable?

And why was my heart beating so fast?

I'd gone too far. That was it. She wanted the regular clichés: candlelit restaurant, sharing popcorn in the movie theater. I had gone off book. But I'd wanted it to be special. The more I got to know Abigail Murrow, the more I realized how much depth she had. Some people were puddles, but she was an ocean.

I wanted to do something that she knew was done specially for her, and her only. I guess I'd crossed a line. This was strictly business, after all.

"If it's too much—"

"It's amazing."

Relief flooded through me. This entire night had been a

tornado of emotions. Trying to create the perfect first date. Trying to be a good friend.

Because that's what we were. Friends. Weren't we? Just friends?

Shut up, shut up, shut up.

Strictly business.

But if it was strictly business, how come Abby was the only girl I had ever thought about doing something like this for?

The opening credits of Killer Klowns from Outer Space played, but I didn't take anything on the screen in. Instead, I was trying not to think of the fact I was sitting close enough to Abby that our arms were touching. I felt way too aware of her presence, her proximity, like the heat you feel when you hold your hand over a stovetop. How easy it would be to reach out and take her hand.

To touch her face.

To kiss her.

Shut up!

"Where did you even think about this?" Abby asked over the crackling voices from my laptop speaker.

"It was Jordyn's idea, kind of."

"Really?"

"Sort of." I was growing close to Abby, but I wasn't sure how honest I wanted to be. From the outside, my family looked like the American Dream. Married eighteen years, two kids, a white picket fence. But appearances could be deceiving. I'd never shared this part of my life with anybody. Should I really be sharing it with my fake girlfriend?

"You don't have to explain if you don't want to," Abby said quickly. She could read me like a book, that girl.

I hesitated. "My parents... they fight a lot. They always have. Always will. They won't get divorced because they're scared of what people will think."

"My mom was like that for a long time."

"Yeah?"

"So much." The image of a giant clown reflected in her eyes.

"When we were kids, Jordie and I took off all the time. We still do. If you knock on our door there's like an eighty percent chance we're not home. It's why I'm always on the football field. Or at parties or social events. Why I know all the best places to go. I take anything that gives me an excuse to not be trapped at home."

Abby's eyes met mine. Her eyes were so green, shining full of empathy.

She understood.

I took a deep breath and continued. "When we were little and they started fighting, I'd hide in Jordyn's room and we'd watch movies on an old laptop. We did it our entire childhood. Once we were old enough, we stopped. Instead, we just stayed out of the house. I'd go to Dylan's, Jordyn went to Hailey's."

"One night last year, mom and dad, they got into it pretty bad. It was two, three in the morning. Jordie woke me up. She needed to get out of the house immediately, but Hailey was at a cheer competition. She didn't know where to go, but she needed to go. Anywhere. Just get away. I thought we'd find a cheap movie somewhere, but the theater was closed. Neither of us wanted to go back home. She was so sad. I can't even… it just felt like the most important thing in the world that I got her to a movie that night. It probably sounds stupid."

"It doesn't," Abby whispered.

"We went to the highway, figured we'd go to the next town and find a movie theater there. But it was too late. Jordie wanted to go back home, but there was no way I was letting her down. We pulled off the freeway and ended up here. All I had was my cell phone and some textbooks. So I stacked the textbooks on the hood, propped up my phone, and we watched Harry Potter until the sun rose and my battery died. It was — is — Jordyn's favorite. The next time my parents got into it, we did the same thing. Only we brought a laptop and some popcorn. Each time they scream, we come here. Each time, it gets a little bigger. Until you get what you see today. A projector and everything."

I paused. That story was the most personal thing I'd told anyone in a long, long time. "And that's the sad history behind the Jones' Family Drive-In."

ABBY

*M*y heart broke like a glass underfoot. Chase was right — the entire time I'd known him, I'd assumed he had the perfect All-American family, the perfect All-American life. I'd seen his parents in the stands at one of his games. They looked so happy together. I thought it was strange that Jordyn wasn't sitting with them. Now I knew why.

"Chase…" I didn't know what to say, so I took his hand. It was cold. "I'm so sorry. Was Jordyn ok with you taking me here?"

Chase swallowed a handful of popcorn. "She thinks you're good for me. She said you looked like Hermione, which from Jordyn is the biggest compliment you can get."

I smiled.

"What, Jones, you had some childhood crush on Emma Watson?" I raised my eyebrows. "Chase Jones, secret Harry Potter nerd?"

"My first crush." He laughed.

I paused for a second. "I know what it's like when parents fight."

"Yeah?"

"My mom was obsessed with being perfect. Me, Katie, my dad — we had to do everything the right way. Her way. I tried to shield Katie from it as much as I could. We always had to look right, to act right. Like we were her little dolls. She was obsessed with how things looked to other people. When I was little, all I wanted was a big, messy Christmas tree. Like in a cartoon. Tinsel and colorful lights and goofy ornaments. But mom didn't like the way it made the house look. So, she let us have two decorations. A Christmas tree with white lights only and tasteful silver ornaments that she put on herself, and a wreath for the front door."

Chase was quiet for a moment.

"Bit of a grinch," he eventually said, softly.

"Huge grinch," I agreed. "But, as hard as we tried, I guess we didn't fit her vision of the perfect family. I don't know if it was dad, or if it was Katie, or if it was me. But she left. She didn't say why. She just went one day. She has a new boyfriend now, he has kids. Feels like she replaced us."

Chase squeezed my hand.

I squeezed back. "She doesn't call much anymore. Just on the days she's supposed to call. Holidays. Birthdays. Milestone events. It's like she's following this list of all the things you're supposed to do if you're a mom. Trying to make sure I'm on track to go to NYU like she did."

We sat in silence for another moment — aside from the random screams from people trying to avoid being murdered by clowns on screen.

I felt Chase's body tense next to mine as he disentangled his hand. I thought for a moment he would leap up, out of the way, and end the date. Take me home. We would drive in silence and pretend this heart-to-heart never happened.

But he didn't. Instead, he leaned back and circled his arm around my shoulder, pulling me close to him.

He didn't say a word.

Neither did I.

If we talked, it might ruin this whole moment. Reality might come crashing in, a freezing wave over a fragile sand castle.

And so, I rested my head on Chase's chest, listening to his heart thump beneath his shirt. His body felt warm, and his arm around my shoulder felt strong. His fingertips absent-mindedly trailed up and down my arm. His touch made me feel dizzy. In a good way.

Such a good way.

The confusion swirling inside me was deafening amidst the silence.

I finally closed my eyes, and then, for a second, I could pretend that this was real.

ABBY

*I*n my dreams, our entire date was like a black and white movie. A full orchestra played, the music crackling like it was on an old record. Chase wore a black suit with a bowtie. A giant sign with flashing lights said "Jones Family Drive-In." He held my hand and led me to my seat. We laughed, we talked, we ate candy. Just as the picture was drawing to a close, he turned to me and took my face in his hand.

I looked deep into his eyes.

Ever so gently, he pulled me towards him.

The music swelled.

Before our lips touched, I woke up.

I was lying in my bed, curled beneath the warm blankets. It was late October. Outside, the trees had all changed color, the maple in our backyard littering the lawn with giant red leaves.

Dad whistled from somewhere in the house. It was a catchy song — I think it came from an old school bubblegum commercial from forever ago.

I tried to ignore the sound, tried to close my eyes and drift back into my dream.

It had been a week since Chase and I's clichéd date. I didn't see Chase much in the past week — he was busy during lunch and after school every day, preparing for a rivalry game against the only other undefeated football team in our school's division.

The game ended up being close, and for once it was Dylan, not Chase, that led the charge, as he plunged into the end zone for the go-ahead touchdown with only three minutes remaining. The defense did their part and Evermore remained undefeated. Still, Click was buzzing this morning with one thing that people apparently wanted to talk about more than Evermore's unbroken winning streak: where was Chase Jones's girlfriend last night at the game? Had they broken up?

The commenters were going wild, and the rumor mill was churning.

The truth was much less glamorous than the speculators on Click would have you believe. In reality, I wanted to be at the game last night, but I wasn't allowed — Dad grounded me for coming home too late after my date. That punishment stretched to include Friday Night Football game appearances.

My additional punishment was almost worse. The morning after the date, Dad sat me — and Katie, despite her protests — down to explain the birds and the bees. The two of us squirmed and cringed through the entire lecture, while our poor dad tried his best to be a good, responsible parent.

As I tried to return to my dream, my stomach grumbled. The smell of sizzling bacon filled the house. Dad's Saturday brunch special. Despite willing myself to return to the dreamy drive-in with my dreamy fake boyfriend, I couldn't fall back asleep. Sigh. Why did the good dreams always end too early? And why was I so obsessed with the idea of kissing Chase?

I flushed at the thought. Last Saturday, in the back of his car, I had an overwhelming longing for him to do just that: kiss me. And I had tried, unsuccessfully, to get the thought out of my head ever since.

I got out of bed and threw on some sweatpants before plodding downstairs. Dad dished up a plate of bacon, eggs, and lightly buttered toast, and set it in front of me.

"So — have you learned your lesson?" He sat at the table across from me, crunched on a piece of burnt bacon, and washed it down with orange juice. Extra pulp, the only kind we ever have in the Murrow household.

"Yes, Dad."

I wore my best 'Apologetic Daughter' face. It was the expression that said that no matter how disappointed he was in me, I was more disappointed in myself. Which was a lie. I would take being grounded for the rest of my life if it meant I got to have another date with Chase.

"Okay. But you have to promise me you'll be more careful." He shook a piece of bacon at me like he was a politician pointing a finger. "I know how easy it is for time to slip away when you're out with your friends."

Dad, despite his progressive nature, had a tough time verbalizing that I had been out too late by myself with A Boy. It was like he thought that if he said it out loud, that would make it real. Not that I blamed him — he was a single dad raising girls. I tried to imagine myself in his shoes by thinking about how protective I was of Katie. I couldn't imagine what I would do if she stayed out past curfew. I wanted to make sure she was safe at all times.

"You are ungrounded," Dad said. "But you still have a curfew. If you break the curfew again without calling, there'll be some punishment."

"Real vague, Dad."

"I'm hoping you just won't break curfew again."

"I won't," I promised.

We finished our breakfast, then I hurried to my room to get ready. Now that I wasn't grounded, I had one thing and one thing only on my mind. I texted Chase and eagerly awaited his reply.

Too eagerly.

It was clear, even to me: I'd developed very real feelings for my very fake boyfriend.

Long story made short: I was screwed.

CHASE

*M*y shoulder was sore, my ribs were bruised, and there was a cut on the back of my hand, but none of that mattered, because I was about to see Abby. As promised, she texted me immediately after her punishment was lifted and we made plans to go for a walk through the city park.

I told myself this would be an excellent opportunity to get seen in public and get some hits on Click to dispel the rumors of our break-up.

That's what I told myself, at least. What my brain wasn't prepared to answer was why, if this was all for appearances, had we chosen the city park to meet up? Somewhere nobody from our school ever hung out. Especially not in the late October chill.

I paced in front of a park bench excitedly. It was the same excitement that coursed through my body in the locker room while I was waiting to take the field for a big game. Around me, the birds sang, and the yellow and orange leaves rustled in the fall wind.

Abby arrived, and I felt my heart accelerate. She was

wearing a grey peacoat and a pink wool hat. The cool wind made her cheeks rosy. Her long, dark hair was loose and shiny, falling around her shoulders.

"Fancy seeing you here," she said.

"I'm happy you escaped prison, finally."

"It was a close call. I had to leave some people behind. It was very sad." She brushed a fake tear from her cheek.

"Is your dad mad at me still?" I couldn't hide the apprehension in my voice.

Last week on our date, we had fallen asleep at the drive-in, her snuggled into me. I don't know what had possessed me to pull her towards me like that. The intensity of the conversation? A gesture of friendship? A sign of solidarity for screwed up families? Maybe.

Or was the real reason that it was the only way I could stop myself from leaning over and kissing her? If I kissed her, it would screw everything up. Abby wanted everything to be strictly business.

Either way, what I had done created an impossibly intimate moment between us. I held her as we fell asleep, her face pressed into my chest. I spent the week worrying that we crossed a line, but neither of us mentioned it. Maybe she wasn't thinking about it as much as I was. The way she felt in my arms, it just felt so... right. Natural.

When we woke, it was hours later. Way after her curfew. I brought her home in a panic, which grew when we arrived and I realized the light was still on in the living room. I walked her to the door, but her dad answered before I said goodbye.

"Good night, Chase," he had said sternly, by way of greeting.

"Sorry, I—"

"Good night."

On the drive home, I told myself that this was only a fake

relationship, so it didn't really matter what Abby's dad thought. But no matter how hard I tried to convince myself that was true, I failed.

"He's not thrilled," Abby said.

"Does he know we're hanging out again?"

"Yep."

My stomach knotted. "And?"

"He's right behind you."

I jumped, but of course, there was no one behind me.

Abby laughed. "You're so nervous!"

"I am not."

"Yes, you are. Oh my — do you think my dad is SCARY?"

"No—"

"You totally do. Chase Jones is scared of my little old dad."

Denial would've only made things worse, so I nodded, laughing.

We followed the paved path through the park, our conversation meandering as much as we did. We talked about football, about her sister, and we each cracked subtle jokes about our relationship.

"I'm excited to see what you write," I said.

She nudged a fallen leaf off the path with the toe of her boot. "Really? I thought you didn't read anything about yourself."

"I'll make an exception for you," I said. "As long as you don't trash me too bad."

She winced. "You must define 'too bad.' I believe the exact sentence I use is 'Chase Jones is an egotistical jerk who only cares about his stats.'"

I laughed. "Well, that's completely true."

"One hundred percent."

Without thinking, I took her hand in mine. Our fingers intertwined naturally, and we pulled closer together. There wasn't anyone around. No one to take pictures. No reason for us to hold hands unless...

"Abby," I said, at the same time as she said "Chase."

We looked at each other for a second, and then I said "You first," at the same time as she said "Go ahead."

She blushed. She looked so cute when she blushed.

"Seriously, you first," I said.

"Oh, uh, never mind." Her blush deepened. "What were you going to say?"

What was I going to say? I had no idea.

"Oh... uh, forget it. Nothing."

We stared at each other for a second, our eyes in an unspoken standoff. What was she thinking? What was she holding back from saying? And why did I care so much?

So much for this being strictly business.

ABBY

"*T*his is insane! You've outdone yourself." I stared at the costume Izzy laid out on my bed. When I told her what I was planning to dress up as for the annual Costume Crawl on Main Street, she marched over to my house with a trunk full of clothes. It was Halloween afternoon, a few hours before the crawl started, and only a few days before Chase and I hit the official three-week mark, as per Click.

"He'll love it," Izzy said. She sprawled on my bed, already dressed up in her Ariana Grande costume, complete with super high ponytail and winged eyeliner. She looked amazing.

"I'm not doing it for him." I looked up from the vanity, where I was attempting to curl my hair. I was doing it for him.

"No, of course not." Sarcasm dripped from her words like honey from a spoon. "You'd NEVER want your boyfriend to think you were hot."

"It's not like that."

So why did I decide to go as Hermione Granger? Chase's self-confessed childhood crush?

Izzy rolled her eyes so hard that I was amazed they stayed in her head. "Yes, your relationship is more evolved than physical appearance. You've transcended the superficial realm of physical attractiveness, and now you are connecting on a strictly soul to soul level."

I pretended to gag. While I maintained a facade of playfulness on the outside, on the inside I was a rollicking storm of turmoil. This was the first time Chase, Izzy, Jordyn, and Dylan would all be hanging out together for an entire night. Like, deliberately. What if I did something wrong? What if they caught on?

"Are we meeting him there?" Izzy asked.

"He's driving Jordyn and Dylan."

"The sister and the best friend," Izzy mused. "A potent combination. Did they ever have a thing? They seem super close."

"I never asked, but I doubt it. Sounds more like they were the Three Musketeers growing up. Chase is pretty laid back, but I think he'd kill Dylan if he ever made a move on Jordyn."

I finished curling my hair and began putting on my costume: grey school uniform complete with shirt, striped tie, grey V-neck sweater, and short, pleated skirt (for necessary sex appeal, Izzy claimed), topped off with a black cape. My hair was perfectly curled, and I clutched a "wand" that was actually a drumstick belonging to Izzy's musician brother, Leo.

"How do I look?" I smiled bashfully. I kinda already knew the costume looked great.

"Stupefying!"

"Then let's go."

♥

MAIN STREET WAS CRAWLING with spooky specters, ghastly ghouls, perfect pumpkins, and terrifying teens. The Monster Mash played and a group of five skeletons breakdanced under a giant inflatable pumpkin that had disco ball lighting. Smiling ghosts hung from the street lamps and it seemed like everyone was wearing an incredible costume. Laughter and shrieks filled the air, and the fall wind carried the scent of melted caramel being poured over fresh apples.

Abby: We're by Peak's.

Chase: On our way.

My heart did the same silly flip it always did when Chase's name appeared on my phone. A minute later, he, Dylan, and Jordyn arrived.

"Abby!" Chase's jaw practically hit the ground when he saw me.

Another point for Abby.

Dylan was dressed as your standard vampire, complete with fake fangs and a trickle of red make up from the corner of his mouth. Chase made for an unbelievably hot pirate with a patch over one eye, a billowing white shirt, and a red bandana. He'd let a five-o'clock shadow grow on his jaw, just the perfect length to make me wonder about how rough it would feel if we —

Stop it, Abby.

Despite Chase's hotness, Jordyn was the one who stole the show.

She wore an Evermore football uniform, and she'd cleverly styled her hair to match the way Chase usually wore his. She also had a medal around her neck. When she saw me, she gave me an enormous hug. "Oh Abigail, how I have missed you in my manly way."

Chase sighed so loudly that I was surprised the entire crowd didn't look. "For Halloween this year, Jordyn thought it would be oh-so-funny to go as me. I drew the line at going as her in return."

"Oh, please, you know it's hilarious," Jordyn said. "Oh look at me, I'm the quarterback, love me love me love me. Watch as I throw this ball REALLY FAR."

Izzy and I both laughed. Dylan looked distinctly uncomfortable. I couldn't blame him — it was eerie how much Jordyn looked like Chase right now.

"Love your costume, you totally give Johnny Depp a run for his money." I said as I gave Chase — the real Chase — a hug.

"You look amazing, seriously." Chase wrapped his arms around me, hugging me for a little longer than was necessary. Not that I was complaining.

"Couldn't have Emma Watson being the focus of my boyfriend's secret weird, nerdy fantasies anymore," I joked. But I wasn't joking.

He slid his hand into mine. "Where to?"

"The same place we go every year!" Izzy shouted. She grabbed Jordyn and Dylan by the wrists and plowed through the crowd.

"Where is she—"

"The fortune teller," I said. "Every year, we go to the fortune teller and get our fortunes read. Usually we just get them to do us by ourselves, but if you're a couple…"

"Ah, so that's why you needed a boyfriend for tonight."

"Among other reasons," I teased. "You're big and strong and can fight off any dark wizards that come after me."

"You can come away with me on my boat — there are no wizards at sea."

"So, the swashbuckling pirate will kidnap me and steal me away from all of this?" I gestured wildly around the Costume Crawl.

"Gladly. And it's not kidnapping if you want to go."

I laughed and untangled my hand from his, curling my arm in his instead. I felt his bicep through his shirt. If he wanted to, he could lift me up like I weighed nothing at all.

Seriously Abby, stop it.

But I didn't want to.

♥

THE FORTUNE TELLER was in a wagon up the street, near the Red Rainbow Diner.

Izzy, Dylan, and Jordyn had already received their fortunes. They were all the perfect kind of vague that you couldn't really refute them even if you wanted to — but you also couldn't use them to actually tell if they came true. Dylan's was my favorite — seek what you want, brave the dragon, and find gold near. For the rest of the night, whenever we asked Dylan to do something, we would tell him he needed to brave the dragon.

Chase and I, as a couple, went to get our fortunes told together. We paid ten dollars to Frankenstein's Monster — a customary rip off price that Chase insisted on paying for — then parted the beaded curtain and stepped inside. The wagon was lit with a black light. There was a crystal ball in the center of the floor with cushions surrounding it. A strange mist rose from beneath it — dry ice, probably. The powerful smell of burning incense made my head feel light.

"You come for guidance," a strange voice said in a low, purposeful baritone. A woman emerged from the darkness. Her eyes were glassy, her cheeks rosy, and she had a large black mole above the corner of her mouth. Her silver jewelry clinked and clanked as she sat on the seat across from us.

"Yes. That." I didn't have Izzy's confidence. A born improvisor, she probably played along perfectly. I felt silly, like if I pretended that I really believed, the fortune teller would start making fun of me. It was a stupid fear, but I couldn't shake it.

The fortune teller made a gesture that I'm sure she thought looked spooky. "Place your hands on the crystal, his hand over yours. The young gentleman's fingers must contact the glass."

I placed my hand on the crystal ball. Chase put his hand over mine. I blushed and was very thankful for the darkness.

She waved her hands over the ball and wiggled her fingers. Mist rolled from beneath the crystal and the dim lighting flickered. Smoke curled and twisted inside the crystal and colors flashed. It was like watching a tiny storm cloud. The fortune teller's voice changed, like she was in a trance.

"Your world is patched; damaged and frail.

A dream dreamed, a dream sought, thrown and veiled.

Two ropes wound, a knot to untie.

But as the world knows, most truth loves the sweet lie."

Her trance disappeared. The storm inside the crystal ball also disappeared.

What the…?

Goosebumps pebbled my arms.

"Let's go," Chase said, shifting from foot to foot. It was difficult to tell with the light, but he looked pale suddenly.

When we left the wagon, Izzy grabbed my arm right away. "I will get my girl some candied apples. We'll be right back."

"We can go together," Chase said, his voice slightly shaky.

"If we go together, how can we talk about you?" Izzy winked, then away we went, Izzy pulling me along.

"What, Iz?" I asked, the second we were out of earshot.

"Uh… Abs… You look like you're about to fall off the planet. Figured I'd steal you away so you can catch your breath. What'd she say that spooked you so bad? That you two would be together forever?"

"Not exactly," I said.

We found the candied apple booth across the street.

"I wouldn't worry about it. Remember when she told me a great tragedy would befall me when the wolf howled and the moon bled? I'm still waiting for that bloody moon. It's been three years." She shook her fist at the moon theatrically. "Bleed, you stupid moon!"

I smiled. Izzy was the one person who could cheer me up no matter how I felt. I paid for our candied apples. My best friend was one of a kind, it was the least I could do.

Izzy suddenly elbowed me in the side. "Well, look what the cat dragged in."

I whirled around to take in a sight that made my heart drop.

Savannah was standing next to Chase. Her red hair cascaded down her shoulders, and her skintight pants were green and shimmery, like the scales of a fish. She wore a loose jacket. She was laughing, and Chase was looking at her with… admiration?

He said something to her, a smile on his lips, and she spun around for him. Her jacket flared as she spun, revealing the seashell bikini top beneath.

"Isn't she cold?" Izzy practically shouted.

"Apparently not," I said. I suddenly felt very plain, dull, and childish in my wizarding get-up. As if Chase Jones would want his girlfriend dressing up as a character from a kids' book on Halloween. What had I been thinking?

Across the road, Savannah finished spinning, and Chase smiled and applauded her costume. He did the gentlemanly thing and kept his eyes on hers, instead of checking out her perfect body. Somehow that almost made it worse.

"She looks good," I said numbly.

"Not as good as you."

No, she didn't look as good as me. She looked better. Far better. Perfect. If Chase Jones would date someone for real, it would be someone like Savannah. Someone who was perfect.

And not someone like me.

CHASE

"'ll see you around," Savannah said, smiling at me before walking away.

"Yeah, maybe," I replied. It was the first time I'd seen Savannah since she dumped me at the beginning of the year, and I was super happy to see her for one reason, and one reason only: closure. She looked great in her costume, but I felt nothing. No spark. No stir of emotion. No butterflies. I may as well have been talking to Dylan. I was officially over her.

Through our entire conversation, I couldn't get Abby and how cute she looked in her Hermione costume out of my head.

She had gone through all that trouble to dress up like that for me... right?

Izzy and Abby returned from getting their apples and we spent the rest of the evening exploring all the attractions the Costume Crawl offered. We cheered from the sidelines during the costume parade, ate way too much candy, and Dylan let a tarantula crawl across his face — something the rest of us wanted no part of.

Through it all, Abby was unusually quiet and frequently took off with Izzy to discuss... something. Me, maybe? Or was that just my ego again? More likely they were discussing Nicholas Applebee, I reasoned.

I tried my best to shake Abby from the funk that had taken hold of her, but no matter how many jokes I told or how ridiculous I acted, I couldn't get more than a pained smile.

What was going on?

ABBY

*N*ovember 4th. Three weeks to the day I started dating Chase. The Friday after the Costume Crawl was a blur of classes and public appearances with Chase. Lunch in the cafeteria, a study session in the library where we laughed so loud we got kicked out, and a peck on the cheek after the Football game. Click went crazy with pictures of us looking happy together.

Which was just what we wanted. We needed to emphasize to the saboteur they needed to bring their 'A' game if they wanted to break us up.

Over the weekend, it got harder and harder to focus. A deadline was looming, a deadline I was dreading. Every morning I looked at my calendar and thought about the three-week countdown.

I was tempted to delete Click, but I suspected that the saboteur would contact me either way. And besides, wasn't that the whole point of my fake relationship? To find out what the saboteur was sending to the girls Chase was actually interested in?

Still, the pit of my stomach was in knots when I thought

about it. The last three weeks had been incredible, like a life that belonged to someone else. It worried me that the second the saboteur sent me anything, Chase would figure it all out quickly, and I would end up being a moment in his past.

November 4th was a Monday, but we didn't have school — something about a development day for teachers. This meant I could wallow in bed in the morning, struggling with my sadness about what was about to unfold. Unfortunately, this meant I would be left to think about Click all day with no distraction. My phone buzzed.

Chase: Anything on Click?

Abby: Nothing yet.

Chase: Keep me posted. Headed to Main Street with Jordyn. Meet up later?

Abby: *salute emoji* I'll be around.

There was no point waiting around my house for a blast from Click, so I went to Main Street early, hoping to casually bump into Chase and Jordyn. I was in the stationery store when my phone buzzed.

Click: You've received an anonymous message. Open? Y/N

A spike of adrenaline shot through me. So, this was it. The saboteur's first move to end my fake relationship with Chase. What could they send that would make me instantly dump Chase?

I nervously swiped the message open.

It was a photo of Chase on Main Street. He was walking with Savannah, his hand around her shoulder. He was pulling her close to him, and her beautiful red hair was falling over his arm. Like a picture from a magazine — two perfect people, walking side by side, united by their beauty. The picture gave me a pang of jealousy immediately. Randomly, I noticed in the picture that there was a cloud in the sky that looked exactly like a duck. I wondered if I had focused on the cloud's strange shape as a coping technique — anything not to think about Chase with her.

The photo was captioned:

He's lying to you. Thought you should know.

Then, before I could examine the photo further, it vanished.

A lump formed in my throat. Chase and Savannah. I mean, he'd been interested in her the entire time — that's why we were doing this, wasn't it? Even if he was actually with her right now, I couldn't be angry. That was the point of our arrangement.

Maybe I'd just read too much into his actions when he had held me to him on our date, when he'd pulled me close. He was just being a good friend. Just trying to give me the perfect fake boyfriend experience. Wasn't he? It was what I'd asked for.

Think, Abby, think. Think about the photo. What did you really see?

Chase with Savannah. They were both wearing jackets, and they'd dated in the summer, so the picture was probably recent. While Chase was recognizable in the photo, technically I'd only seen the back of the girl's head. It might not have been Savannah. But if not, who could it be? That gorgeous red hair was unmistakable.

Was there anything else in the photo that stuck out?

I texted Chase.

Abby: Someone sent me a photo. You and Savannah.

As I waited for a reply, I tilted my head back and looked at the sky.

There was a cloud shaped like a duck. A duck!

Just like in the photo.

Whoever was responsible had taken the picture TODAY.

I took off, running as fast as my stubby legs could carry me. My phone buzzed in my pocket, but I ignored it. If I

143

hurried, I could catch Madison, put her indisputably at the scene of the crime. Or I'd see Chase with Savannah and I'd know the photo was real. Or maybe I'd see something else entirely.

My lungs heaved.

My legs felt like they would give out.

I arrived at the top of Main Street after what seemed like an eternity. I collapsed on a bench outside Peak's to catch my breath.

Once I could breathe again, I looked around, trying to find one of my suspects. The area was busy, but there was no sign of Chase, Savannah, or Madison.

I swore.

"Abby?"

I looked at the couple eating frozen yogurt on the bench across from me. It was Nicholas and Payton. They both had their tablets open, and they were comparing photos from last week's football game. Evermore's undefeated season was the sole focus of the Pinnacle right now.

Embarrassed as I was with Payton and Nicholas catching me red faced, sweaty and swearing, I realized that I didn't care that Payton and Nicholas were here together. They looked good together, in fact. My crush on Nicholas was ancient history, that much was clear to me.

"Have you seen Madison Albright?" I asked between breaths.

Nicholas shook his head.

"I did," Payton said. "A few minutes ago."

"Where?!" I practically yelled. "What was she doing?"

"Uhh… she was just walking down Main, on her phone."

Sweet vindication.

"Talking to someone?"

Payton shook her head. "I think she was taking a photo, maybe a selfie or something."

Yes.

Yes, yes, yes.

"And Chase?" I asked, my breath slowly returning. "Have you seen Chase?"

"No, sorry, Abby." Payton shook her head.

"Shouldn't you... I mean aren't you...?" Nicholas fumbled.

"Yes." I cut through his mumbles with the answer to the question I knew he was asking.

I checked my phone.

Chase: From when?

30

CHASE

*A*bby: Meet me at Peak's.

My heart raced. If the saboteur had sent a photo of me and Savannah to Abby, what did they send to Savannah? The one I was supposedly kissing someone in... could it be photos of me and a different ex the saboteur was circulating? For the millionth time in my life, I cursed Click. The platform was designed to drive gossip and drama, and as the quarterback, I was the center of much of the unwanted attention.

"Verdict?" Jordyn stood beside me. Our parents were fighting again this morning, leaving both of us desperate to get out of the house.

"We need to meet Abby at Peak's."

Jordyn smiled. "Even in November, I won't turn down frozen yogurt."

She liked Abby. She said I was happy lately.

She was right.

We were at the other end of Main Street when Abby texted, so it took us a good ten minutes to get to Peak's. When we arrived, Abby was sitting on one of the benches, her phone out. It looked like she was writing notes. I smiled to myself — she was always taking notes. She said it was the key to being a great journalist.

Her eyes flitted to me, then to my sister. "Jordyn."

"What. Is. Up." Jordyn gave her a fist bump.

"And what am I? Chopped liver?" I tried to joke, but the words sounded more bitter than I meant.

Abby ignored my question and addressed Jordyn directly. "You two were together all morning?"

"We were bored. Had to get out of the house," Jordyn said. "And I must say, my morning just got a lot more interesting. I hear Click is throwing a tantrum?"

Abby filled us in. Someone had sent her a picture of me with Savannah. Judging from the photo, they took the picture today. Which was impossible — I hadn't seen Savannah since the Costume Crawl. Even at school she tried to avoid me. Payton, the football reporter, spotted Madison in the area. Was my ex-girlfriend stalking me? I didn't like the idea, but I couldn't deny the possibility that Madison would use Click to destroy my life. It was very much a Madi move. She didn't want me anymore, but she sure didn't want anyone else to have me either.

After Abby finished, Jordyn spoke.

"Well. I can tell you I was with Chase the whole morning. Haven't seen Savannah other than the Costume Crawl. She kinda bailed on Chase in a hurry without giving him any chance to explain himself."

There she goes again, I thought. Being just a little over-protective and accusing people of bailing on me. I guess our overprotective twin relationship truly went both ways.

"Did Chase put his arm around you today?" Abby asked.

I thought about it and answered before Jordyn did. "Once. I gave her like a half-hug after she complained that I wouldn't let her eat frozen yogurt for breakfast."

Jordyn gasped, pretending to be offended. "Pretty sure you have that backwards, Mr. Have You Tried The Birthday Cake With Peanut Butter Cups?"

Abby laughed. The sound was light and musical, and it filled me with warmth.

"So most likely scenario — Photoshop?"

I sighed and ran my hands through my hair. Faking pictures of me was low, even for Madison. "So, what now? Should I go talk to Madison?"

Jordyn cracked her knuckles. "Let me."

"I want her disciplined, not dead."

"Dead is a type of discipline."

Abby smirked at our banter. "What we need is proof. It seems like there's a ninety percent chance that it involves Madison, but we can't do anything until we know for sure. We need to catch her in the act."

"How?" I looked at Abby, like she would have an answer prepared, but she shrugged.

"Great question."

Jordyn glanced between Abby and I, seeming to read something. She stretched dramatically. She was not a natural actress. "And while you two try to figure that out, I will go for a wander. Catch you later."

"Bye." Abby smiled and waited for her to leave. "Does she know the truth about us now? Did you tell her?"

Good question. I hadn't been able to bring myself to tell Jordyn the truth, especially with how psyched she was about me being with Abby. She loved her, and I mean, it made sense. Abby was great.

I shook my head. "No. I told her someone was sabotaging my relationships, and I told her you knew that too, and believed me, not the saboteur. She thinks this is for real with us. And she likes you for standing up for me, believing in me. I still haven't told anyone the truth... have you?"

Abby shook her head, and I smiled, holding out my hand for her to take it. I felt glad. Somehow, I didn't like the thought of anyone knowing this was fake. If nobody knew, it made it easier to pretend…

"So, I guess we're still fake dating?" Abby brought me back to reality, away from any pretense I had just been imagining. "I mean, we need to look like we argued, but stayed together, so the saboteur strikes again. This will be the first time they didn't get the job done in one go. They're gonna be maaaaaad!"

We were on the right track, one step closer to catching the saboteur. So why did I feel so sad about it?

I spent the next hour strolling down Main Street with Abby. We dipped in and out of stores, grabbed some snacks, and plotted different ways to catch Madison. It would be challenging. Abby was convinced that Madison was laying the groundwork for something larger. If she wanted Abby to break up with me, she'd need to send more than a photo of me with Savannah.

However, we couldn't act like nothing happened, either. We decided we had to create some artificial distance between us so that Madison would believe we were falling for her tricks. We wanted to encourage her, to hopefully draw her out so we could catch her in the act.

I walked Abby back to her car.

When we arrived at her vehicle, she stopped for a second, pausing with her hand on the door handle.

"It would've been okay," she said.

"Huh?"

"If it had been you and Savannah in the pic, if it was taken today. Like for real."

I didn't know what to say.

"That's the whole point, isn't it?" she said. "Find out who is sabotaging your relationships so you could date Savannah?

But if you were with Savannah already without finding out, that would just be a bonus. Get her back in advance. We can still work on catching the saboteur in the meantime."

She was right. That was the point. And it was my fault that I'd taken things more seriously than that. "And so you can write the social feature and make Nicholas like you."

"Right," she agreed, looking away. What wasn't she telling me?

"So, I guess, as long as we are still dating and you still have an article to write... what's next on your checklist?"

"Christmas Crush invite."

"Still want it big and in public?"

"Don't really care," Abby said. "Just want to make sure someone invites me to a dance before I'm old, withered, and surrounded by cats."

"I'll see what I can do," I said, laughing.

She got in her car, and I watched her drive away.

I was left scratching my head. She said it wouldn't bother her if I was with Savannah.

I was an idiot for even thinking for a second we might be something more than what we were.

When I got home, I planned to sit down, stare in the mirror, and tell myself again that for Abby, this was all Strictly Business. She liked intellectual guys; not dumb jocks like me. That's what I was to her: A pawn. Friends or not underneath it all, she was just using our fake relationship for access to social climbing.

Nothing more.

31

CHASE

With November came the first snowfall of the season. Football practice was a nightmare. The ball was tougher to hold, hits hurt a little more, and my arms were numb from the cold. We were gearing up for play-offs, and practice forced me to spend most of my time away from Abby. We were still officially fake-dating — the saboteur was yet to strike again. I was glad they were taking their time, whoever they were. I didn't want to think about breaking up with Abby.

I mean, not that it would be a real break up, but still.

I thought about telling Abby the truth, that I was over Savannah. I mean, Savannah wasn't even mad at me anymore. I didn't really care if I got my explanation or not about who had sabotaged us. But somehow, every time I thought about telling Abby... I couldn't. It would make things weird for her, and put our weird pact on a new, uneven playing field. Abby still needed me to get her social feature written, and I didn't want to screw that up by blurting out the truth.

The Pinnacle's office was near the back of the Fine Arts

Building. Both the office and everyone inside smelled of strong coffee. Abby wasn't there. Before arriving, I'd confirmed with Izzy that she was busy.

Which made this the perfect time to launch Operation Christmas Crush Invite — the next thing on the list.

Aside from Abby, the only person I knew who worked on the Pinnacle staff was Payton. She'd interviewed me a few times when writing articles on the football team, and she was always at the same parties I went to. When I arrived, she was working at a table in the corner, adjusting the layout of the next edition with a geeky-looking guy I assumed was the lead editor.

Was this Nicholas Applebee? My competition?

My expression darkened as I sized the nerdy guy up.

"Hey, Payton, can I steal you for a second?" I asked, trying to keep my tone sweeter than my thoughts.

She smiled and practically skipped away from the table. "What's up?"

"You know how I'm dating Abby, right?"

"You're all over Click. It's almost disgusting."

"It's not the best," I agreed. "Look, anyway, I want to ask her to the Christmas Crush. And I know that she wants it to be personal."

Payton held up her hand. "If you're thinking about asking her through a written ad in the Pinnacle, know we have a strict no-asking-people-out policy. It gets super awkward. It's almost as bad as a public proposal."

"I had something different in mind." I reached into my backpack, pulled out a string of Christmas lights, and explained my plan.

Payton eyed me curiously. She looked impressed. "What do you need from me?"

"This." I pulled out a piece of paper. It was a fake article I'd written announcing Abby's acceptance of my Christmas

Crush invite. It wasn't very good — writing was Abby's thing, not mine. But I had thought long and hard about what I should do, and this was it. Abby would love the gesture.

"I need to make this look like the front page of a newspaper. And that's where you come in." I looked at Payton hopefully as she took the piece of paper from me and skimmed it.

"Chase, this is legit cute. You must really like her."

"It's no big deal," I lied. When I agreed to the fake relationship with Abby, one of her terms was that she wanted a big Christmas Crush invite. The problem with most invites, I decided, was that they were temporary. Someone decorated your car, you said yes, and then took the decorations down. I wanted to create the fake newspaper article because Abby would then have a souvenir. Something to remember this by. She was sentimental, she loved grand gestures. This had to work.

"Can you do it?"

"Would've been easier if you sent an email," Payton said. "Then I wouldn't have to decipher your chicken scratch. But yes, I can do it. But you owe me, Chase. You owe me big."

ABBY

I read the text again.

Chase: Meet me at the football field at 5:30?

I paced through the Pinnacle office, a cup of decaf in my hand. Chase and I had talked little this week. Between my work on the social feature, other editorial tasks, and the monthly call from mom, I simply didn't have time. I still felt a twinge of jealousy whenever I thought about the picture of him with Savannah. Even though the picture was fake, I remembered the way he looked at her during the Costume Crawl. It was a stark reminder that he was only in this so he could prove Madison was the saboteur and then have his life return to normal. It made me sad and angry. Even though he had done nothing wrong — he was just living up to our pact. But even a wonderful fake boyfriend was still a fake.

And yet, it was tough to imagine that he was faking everything. I'd fallen asleep with my head on his chest at the Jones Family Drive-In. I'd felt him running his hand over my arm. We'd held hands when no one was around. He'd planned spectacular dates for me — above and beyond what even a real boyfriend would do. Was that all fake?

I didn't know. I'd never had an actual boyfriend.

I didn't want to think about it. A fake relationship dissolved into pieces if you thought about it too hard. That's why I'd been trying to ignore reality. That's why I'd been doing the same thing mom did when something wasn't perfect — burying myself in my work.

At 5:25, I threw on my jacket and wrapped my scarf around my neck. The sun had already set. The sky was dark. A handful of students scurried through the quad, snow swirling around them. Ice crunched beneath my boots as I walked to the football field, the wind nipping at my cheeks.

Chase sat alone on the creaking metal bleachers, looking gorgeous in his parka and dark hat. Why did he always have to look so effortlessly hot?

The field was lightly dusted with white — the grounds crew tried to keep it mostly clear for the players to practice, but right now there was a fresh sheet of snow blanketing the grass.

"You couldn't pick somewhere warmer to meet, hey?" I asked, shivering.

"Not for this." He dusted off a spot on the bleachers next to him. "You'll want to be sitting for this."

Was that good or bad?

I sat next to him. My heart felt heavy. I braced myself for the knockout blow.

He squinted against the wind. "I hoped it would be nicer out for this. I wanted to make it so you'd remember."

"Remember what?"

"Here." He gave me a small remote with a silver switch.

"And this is?"

He grinned. "Flick the switch."

"I don't know what you have up your sleeve, Chase Jones." My curiosity easily got the better of me. I flipped the switch.

My name appeared beneath the snow, lit in blue, green,

red, and gold. Christmas lights. One by one, colorful letters came to life. When they were finished, a message glowed across the football field:

Abigail Murrow, will you be my Christmas Crush?

My jaw dropped right through the bleachers and a thousand butterflies escaped my stomach. The lights danced, the snow sparkling with a rainbow of colors. Despite the cold, I never wanted the moment to end. I felt a twinge of sadness. How could something so spectacular be fake?

"You did it," I whispered.

"Is that an answer?"

What was I supposed to say? Technically, our checklist meant he only had to invite me to the Christmas Crush. He didn't have to take me. Was he just completing the last step? If he was, I owed him the right answer. It took two to make a fake relationship work.

"Yes," I said. My voice was so soft I thought it was lost in the wind.

Chase put his arm around me.

"This is amazing," I said.

"I had some help from Dylan and Jordyn. Took a lot of work to set up the lights. And before I forget, there's this." He pulled a roll of paper out of his jacket and gave it to me.

I slid the elastic off.

It was a copy of the Pinnacle.

No, it was different.

The headline read: Abby and Chase Crush Christmas. There was a small article attached along with a picture of us at the Costume Crawl.

My heart soared. He had gone to all this trouble for me?

"Something to remember me by," Chase said.

Something to remember him by... past tense. Remember. As in, when he's gone. When this is over. When real life returns.

My heart hit the ground with a thump.

My phone buzzed. It was another anonymous message from Click. I didn't want to check it. Not yet… I just wanted one more moment.

As the lights danced across the field, I rested my head on Chase's shoulder and pretended our relationship would never end.

CHASE

*W*e came into the state quarterfinals as heavy favorites. After an ugly back-and-forth affair in the snow, we emerged victorious, but we paid a heavy price. Dylan dislocated his shoulder on a run late in the fourth quarter. Adam caught the go-ahead touchdown, but landed awkwardly and was now limping around on crutches with a high ankle sprain. They were both done for the season.

I set my helmet on the bench beside me. There were streaks of yellow on the black from where the paint had scuffed from a linebacker's helmet during back-to-back sacks. Rock music blared through the locker room.

I shut my eyes, my head throbbing. My body felt like I'd ran full speed into a concrete wall. I had so many injuries I couldn't pick one to focus on, they all just blurred together. Still wearing my equipment, I pulled my phone out of my jacket pocket. It was hard to curl my fingers — I'd slammed my hand into someone's helmet while making a pass under pressure. Were they broken? Sprained? Bruised?

I didn't know. The only thing I knew was that, as low

energy as I was, I was looking forward to seeing Abby after the game. As our fake relationship drew to a close, things were getting awkward between us. The friendly banter that I enjoyed so much felt forced and I couldn't figure out why. Though she denied it, she was keeping her distance. Before, she would welcome me into her home. But now it felt like I was left out in the cold and dark, staring through the window at the warmth inside.

I felt like I was losing her. And this time I didn't feel like I could blame some anonymous saboteur. This time it felt like it was my fault. But I didn't know what I'd done.

I unlocked my phone.

Chase: Did you stick around?

Abby: Close game. You okay? Looked rough down there.

Chase: Just a flesh wound.

Now what? Did I invite her out? I wanted to see her. Even if it was just as a friend. I always wanted her around, always wanted her laughing. But I didn't want to put too much pressure on her. I closed my eyes. I would gladly take another dozen bone-crushing hits if they would jiggle loose the part of my brain that could understand girls. I settled for a neutral tone.

Chase: Some guys and I are going to hit Main Street to celebrate, hitting up the diner. You want to come?

I changed out of my equipment and took a quick shower — made even more difficult by my inability to close my swollen fist around the shampoo bottle. When I was finished, I had a text from Abby waiting for me.

Abby: It's okay, you've done your part. And don't worry, I'll be out of your hair soon. Just have to figure out what Madison is up to!

I locked my phone without replying to her. What was I going to do, beg her to come? Hardly.

I got dressed slowly, wincing at the pain throbbing through my hand.

I'd done my part? What exactly was that supposed to mean? Was she referring to the checklist? Was our relationship officially over now that we no longer had events that she needed me for?

I tried to fight away the thoughts that gnawed at my mind. Maybe I was wrong to let my feelings get involved in all of this. For Abby, this was just strictly business. I don't know why I had to keep reminding myself of this fact.

I was the last person to leave the locker room.

ABBY

I drove home from the game in near silence, snow falling gently outside the comfortable confines of my car window. The only sounds were the steady scrape of my wipers streaking across the window and Izzy's chattering teeth as she tried to make conversation.

She turned up the heat and rubbed her fingers near the fan. "You don't know it was from him."

I'd lost count of how many times we'd had this conversation since the anonymous blast from Click. "It was his writing," I said. "I'd recognize it anywhere."

"But you don't KNOW. How long did you have the picture for?"

"Long enough," I snapped. Izzy was doing everything in her power to cheer me up, but it wasn't happening.

After leaving the bleachers with Chase a few days before, I had returned to the safety and solitude of my car and opened the message from Click. I expected another photoshopped picture of him locking lips with another girl. What I had actually received from the saboteur was a love letter Chase wrote to Savannah.

That one was a punch to the gut. Chase's handwriting was easily recognizable, and in the background, I saw big bay windows that overlooked the mountains. It was snowing outside when the picture was taken. And the only place in school that had windows like that was the dance studio in the Fine Arts Building.

Possibly against my better judgement, I hadn't been able to tell Chase about the second Click message. I was too scared it was real. I had no idea where the lines overlapped between reality and our sham of a relationship anymore, and I was tired.

"Her name wasn't even on the letter." Izzy persisted.

"There was a giant S at the top," I said. "It was found in the dance studio. And his name was on it. It literally said 'Love, Chase' at the bottom."

"But surely this could be like the time someone sent a picture of him with Savannah. Then it turned out he was with Jordyn all morning."

But was he?

I didn't want to doubt him. I didn't want to doubt Jordyn. But during the Costume Crawl I'd seen the way he looked at Savannah. Like she was perfect. He'd even used the word 'perfect' in his letter to her. Three times, in fact. More than he'd ever said it to me. More than he ever would say it to me.

And the worst part?

As much as I wanted to be angry, I couldn't find the energy. We started our fake relationship with the explicit goal of uncovering the saboteur so that he could explain things to Savannah and be with her. He'd never lied about that. It was even in our contract. What was I supposed to say? He'd held up his end of the bargain. Now I had to hold up mine. I wasn't his girlfriend, not really, but I could still be a friend.

We arrived back at my house. Dad had forgotten to leave the porch light on, so my home was dark and dead.

"Maybe you're right. Maybe it's another fake," I said, not really believing it. There was no doubt in my mind the message had come from the saboteur. But I highly doubted anyone was that good at forging Chase's writing to fool me... what it seemed is that Madison had found a real piece of evidence for once, and she was using it to her advantage. Add in how Chase had looked at Savannah at the Costume Crawl, how perfect she was, and how perfect I wasn't? It was clear what was happening.

"But if it's a fake, we still need to figure out how Madison's connected." I hadn't come clean to Izzy about my fake relationship — that was the kind of thing you kept even from your best friend. But I needed her to work with me.

"What time did you receive the Click?"

"Around 5:45."

"So, let's find out what Madison was doing at 5:45." Izzy scrolled through a dozen of different social media profiles set up by the Queen Bee of Evermore.

"What do you think you're going to find?"

"A post around the same time. If we find a post, that means she had her phone. If she had her phone, she could've sent the Click." Izzy scrunched her face. "Wait."

"What?"

"Look."

It was a live video from a cheerleading competition, held the same day Chase asked me to the Christmas Crush. All of the cheerleaders were there, with Madison proudly on top of the pyramid, her dazzling eyes flashing triumphantly.

"And?"

"Check out the clock."

In the background of the video, there was a clock on the

gym wall. In big red numbers it said 5:43. The video was over five minutes long.

"I don't know who sent you that Click," Izzy said, "but Madison didn't have her phone, and you can't pre-schedule blasts."

"That doesn't mean she's not behind it. She could have had someone send it on her behalf."

"Maybe," Izzy said. She sounded skeptical. "But Madison's pretty much only friends with other cheerleaders. And they're all prancing around with her."

She was right, but I wasn't convinced.

Madison was the saboteur.

I was sure of it.

35

ABBY

*M*adison was behind everything. It made perfect sense. The jaded ex-girlfriend wanted to stop her former boyfriend from being happy. It was such a cliché, but sometimes clichés were clichés for a reason. If I'd learned anything from my years of studying investigative journalists, it was that nine times out of ten, they found the truth in the most obvious answer. However, just because you knew something was true didn't mean you could go around making false accusations and stirring up drama.

No, we had to set a trap and catch Madison in the act.

But how?

"Steal her phone," Izzy suggested. We were meandering along the Riverwalk. It was just below freezing and snow clung to the banks. The patios were empty, furniture moved inside for the year, and the only sound was the gurgling of icy river water.

"Even if I got my hands on her phone, it'd be locked. She could just use Find My Device and brick it before we found anything. Or she could trace it to my house. Think about how that would look on Click — Chase Jones's new girlfriend steals his ex-girlfriend's phone." I shuddered at the thought. To say the last few days had been difficult was putting it mildly. I felt like Chase was getting impatient. He kept asking questions about the saboteur, questions I couldn't answer. He wanted this all to be over so he could get together with Savannah. He never said that, of course. When I asked about Savannah, he was dismissive just to protect my feelings.

Did he know I had feelings for him?

Real feelings?

I sipped my hot chocolate. It was rich and sweet. "How can we lure Madison into the open? She's so careful. It feels like she's always a step ahead. Maybe we can find out who sent the Click blast when she was busy during her cheer competition."

Izzy shook her head. "Could have been anyone. If it wasn't one of Madison's friends, then it was someone she blackmailed. There's not a person in Evermore who will turn on Madison. Not for either of us."

She was right.

"What about Click?" I asked. "Maybe they have a way of tracking who's sending messages to who."

"Not a chance," Izzy replied. She finished her hot chocolate. "Click's built on being anonymous. The whole point of that stupid app is that you can't track anything. Unless she makes a mistake and signs into her own account to send blasts — and given she's the queen of Click, that seems unlikely — there's no way to track anything."

I sighed. That stupid app was becoming the bane of my existence. It made gossip too easy to spread. Too hard to stop. I briefly considered trying to fight fire with fire and blasting Madison's account with pictures of me and Chase, but dismissed the thought. I was not starting an online turf war over a boy I was fake dating. Besides, Chase had seen enough of Click for a lifetime.

I brushed snow off a railing and leaned over it, watching the dark river water foam and churn. It felt like Madison was unbeatable.

"There's no way to prove it's her," I said.

Izzy put her arm around me. "No, not while you two are together. You'll just have to stand—"

"Wait," I said.

"What?"

"Madison wants Chase to be single. That's why she keeps trying to sabotage his relationships. So why does she want him to be single?"

"Because she's a b—"

"Because," I said, cutting Izzy off, "she probably still loves Chase. She wants to be with him. But she won't make a move while he's in a relationship. She thinks if she ends enough of his relationships, he'll come crawling back to her."

Izzy looked doubtful. "I don't think Madison really cares if he's in a relationship or not."

"As a person? No," I agreed. "But as someone who's trying to cultivate a very specific appearance? If she steals Chase away, she looks like the villain. But if Chase comes back to her on his own, then she's the sweet hero who takes in the stray puppy."

Concern flickered across Izzy's face. "Abs, you're scaring me a bit. This doesn't make sense. Chase has been single before and Madison didn't make a move. This doesn't add up."

I dismissed my friend's concern. "It doesn't matter. If Chase is single, odds are whoever's been trying to sabotage our relationship will make a move. We just have to…"

Izzy finished my sentence for me. "You'd have to break up."

Break up. The words hung in the surrounding air, colder than the freezing river. My chest hurt. Was this really the only way? Was I wrong? What if Izzy was right? What if we broke up and Madison didn't make a move? Then I'd be left without Chase and without proof that Madison was the saboteur.

"Seriously, Abs, are you okay?" Izzy looked frightened. "Think about what you're saying. You're going to stage a fake break up with your boyfriend to lure some mystery saboteur out into the open — which might not even happen. It just... it doesn't seem like it will work. I think a lot of people will get hurt."

"I'm open to better suggestions," I said softly. What Izzy didn't know was that it would be a real break up with my fake boyfriend, not the other way round.

"At least you need to talk to Chase first," she said.

I agreed. Even if my plan didn't work, even if the saboteur didn't show themselves, at least Chase would have the chance to restart things with the girl he really wanted.

As much as the thought hurt my heart, I knew it was the right thing to do. I had to talk to my fake boyfriend about our real break up.

36

CHASE

I read the text from Abby again.

And again.

Four simple words:

We need to talk.

How could four words provoke so much dread? We weren't even — technically — in an actual relationship. So why was I dreading our next meeting so much?

I sat in my Jeep in the school parking lot. Cars pulled in and out, their tires splashing through November slush. Ads blared from the radio, one of them advertising a music festival next June.

Finally, after an eternity of waiting, I saw Abby trudge across the parking lot. She smiled sadly as she climbed in the passenger seat, her breath fogging the window.

"I got your text," I said dumbly. I didn't know what else to say.

"Thanks for meeting me." Her tone was kind but formal. The tone coach used when he was benching you for the rest of the game. The tone someone used when you were being replaced.

I smiled weakly. "It's that bad, huh?"

"I think we can lure Madison out," she replied.

"That sounds like good news."

"It is. If we can find proof, then we can both move on." She didn't look at me as she said this, instead turning and staring out the window at the dismal grey afternoon.

Her words echoed in my mind. We can both move on. So this was it, then. After this, she was done with me. Maybe I'd never been more than a checklist to her. Maybe that was all I could ever be to anyone — a box to be ticked. How many of my "friends" felt the same way? How many people were just pretending to be friends for the perks? Abby had pretended to be my girlfriend to get access to parties, but at least she'd been honest about it. That did little to simmer the anger I felt welling in my chest.

"How?" I asked, keeping my tone level.

She rubbed something from her eyes. "By breaking up."

ABBY

*S*ilence never felt so loud. It filled the Jeep, a presence pressing on everything. I felt like I was being crushed. Instinctively, I pulled my feet towards my chest, careful to prevent my wet boots from getting on the seat. I wanted to curl into a ball and hide. Why had I ever thought this fake relationship was a good idea? Even a fake relationship needed to end.

"Okay," Chase said. His voice was cold. He stared straight ahead, his hands at 10 and 2 on the wheel even though we weren't going anywhere. "So, we break up. What then?"

I took a deep breath to keep my voice from hitching. "After we break up, Madison will come to you. She'll try to comfort you and get back together with you."

"Why will she come for me now? She hasn't any of the other times."

I'd thought about this a lot. "Those other times she was trying to hurt you. But our relationship lasted longer than three weeks. It looked to the outside world that it was serious. This time, I suspect she thought she might actually lose you. I don't think she'll take that risk again."

Chase didn't say anything.

What was he thinking?

I would have given anything to be inside his mind at that moment. His perfect face gave nothing away. His eyes were hard and shiny — impossible to read.

"What if she doesn't?"

"Even if she doesn't, you have enough proof."

"Proof?"

"That someone's trying to sabotage your relationships," I said. "We know about the photoshopped photo of you with another girl. We know that the saboteur is using Click to mess up your relationships."

"But we already knew that," he snapped. "How does that help?"

"Because I'll verify it," I said, keeping my voice calm even though fractures were spider webbing across my heart. "When you tell Savannah tell her it happened to me and you too. And I'll explain everything. It… it might not be enough. But I think if she trusts you… I think she'll understand. You guys are talking again, right? So, she is in a somewhat forgiving mood already."

Chase rested his head on the steering wheel for a moment, his eyes closed, his shoulders slumped. It was the same body posture he had after throwing an interception, a look of angry defeat. He didn't think this would work. He thought we'd gone through all of this and that I wasn't delivering my part of the bargain. How could I make him see? How could I make him understand?

"I'm sorry," I said. All the words were in my head, but I couldn't seem to get them out. "I tried; I really did. It's not perfect… but it's the best I can do."

He gently banged his head against the steering wheel. "Okay. So how do we break up?"

ABBY

*M*y neck was in the guillotine, and I was waiting for the blade to drop. Stiff wind whipped my face and puddles of slush pooled around my boots. Nearby, a handful of students threw snowballs at each other. Above, the sky was grey. It felt like it had been forever since I'd seen the sun. The weather matched my mood.

I stood in the center of the quad, Chase's hoodie in my hands. I held it close. It was probably the last piece of Chase I'd ever have. Yesterday, sitting in his Jeep in the parking lot, we'd agreed to break up. It had to be done in public so it could be blasted on Click. We would put our most vulnerable selves out in the world to be seen by everyone.

We'd agreed that I would give him one of his hoodies in the quad, like I was giving it back to him. It would read unmistakably as a break up to any passers-by. He handed me the one he was wearing — his Panthers football hoodie — and I stowed it in my backpack before exiting his Jeep.

I cradled the hoodie. It still smelled like Chase's cologne.

What I would never confess to Chase is that last night, I had worn his hoodie to bed, and cried. It was my last night as

Chase Jones's girlfriend, and the sadness had become impossible to keep bottled up inside me.

The rumor mill was cranking already. After I'd left his Jeep yesterday, Click put us on blast. There was a brief clip of me leaving his vehicle, walking through the parking lot, and rubbing my eyes. The caption: Trouble in Paradise? Immediately after receiving the blast, I got a text from Izzy asking if everything was okay. I just answered a simple "Yes", but didn't say anything else.

I breathed in deeply. It was time to steel my nerves and prepare myself. If my break up would be all over Click, I would not show any weakness. I wouldn't spend the next two years of my life as a sobbing meme.

It's okay, Abby. You're just playing your part. This is your job as a journalist.

You got what you wanted out of this.

Did I?

CHASE

*M*y feet were anchors dragging across the frozen ground. I held a crumpled piece of paper, the original checklist Abby created for us. I'd added a final box:

Break up.

This was the last thing I wanted to do, but Abby was sure it would draw out the saboteur. She was convinced it was Madison who was screwing with me, and this was the only way to confirm it. Plus, she'd completed her checklist. There was no need for her to keep me in her life anymore. My usefulness to her was officially over.

I couldn't eat supper when I got home last night. My parents didn't notice, but Jordyn did. She knocked on my door while I was listening to music — which was much better than her usual habit of barging in uninvited.

"What's wrong?" she asked matter-of-factly.

"Nothing."

"So, Abby?"

I reluctantly removed my headphones. "It's all good."

"Why don't you tell me what's going on, and I can tell you how you're being stupid and how you can stop being stupid?"

That was Jordyn, equal parts caring and blunt. I wanted to tell her the truth. How our entire relationship started off as fake to find out who was sabotaging me. But now I had feelings I couldn't deny. But they weren't reciprocated.

How could I tell her that? Her and Dylan were the two people I never lied to, and I'd lied to both of them about dating Abby. Now what? Admit it to both of them, right when I needed their support the most?

Dylan might understand, but Jordyn? I was worried she would instinctively take my side and she would hate Abby for the rest of her life, even if it was undeserved. I refused to put Abby in that position. I hoped we could form some kind of friendship after everything was said and done. Maybe I was being naïve. Abby wasn't really friends with people like me. And the breakup was her idea. She was gently pushing me out of her life.

"It's complicated," I said.

"So uncomplicate it."

"I can't."

"Try, Chase." She was glaring at me.

"Thanks for the advice," I mumbled. I put my earbuds back in.

Jordyn ripped them out, her blue eyes flashing angrily. "Are you serious right now?"

"What do you want me to say?" I asked, annoyed.

"You like her?"

"What do you think?"

"It doesn't matter what I think," Jordyn snapped. "It matters what she thinks. Does she know how much you like her?"

"I mean I am dating her, I'm sure that conveys I like her." No one — not even Madison — could push my buttons better than Jordyn. She'd never admit it, but she'd mastered mom's snippy tone. "I would like to think she knows."

"Unless you're being a moron," Jordyn said. "And let's be honest — you have moron tendencies when it comes to girls."

"Dude — leave me alone." I used the word on purpose. Jordyn hated when I called her dude, but she was annoying me right now.

"I'm trying to help you."

"Then leave me alone."

"Fine." Jordyn threw the earbuds in my face. "But if I find out you did something irredeemably moronic, I know where you live. And I will punch you."

She slammed the door behind her.

"Thanks for the support," I shouted.

The sight of Abby standing in the center of the quad wiped all memory and all thought from my mind.

Was it really too late?

ABBY

$\mathcal{C}$hase marched over to me, a man on a mission. His expression was grim, the twinkle in his eyes gone. This was not the happy Chase Jones I'd grown to care for over our time together. This was not the Chase Jones I knew. His lips were pressed tight together. He gave me a curt nod, but he couldn't keep eye contact.

"Here." My voice nearly broke as I held out his hoodie. I sensed the people watching us. Students I couldn't name were discreetly holding up their phones to capture the moment for Click. The countdown had started; they were pressing record and waiting for the explosion.

Chase reluctantly took the hoodie.

"So we're doing this," he said, his voice too quiet for anyone but me to hear.

He was playing his role perfectly. His eyes were cold, and he looked miserable as he cradled his hoodie in his hands.

"We had to wake up sometime," I whispered. Yes, Abby — you had to wake up and realize that you had feelings for a boy that only started dating you so you could help him make up with another girl. His love letter to Savannah popped in my mind, the phrases burned in my memory. She was perfect for him. They were perfect for each other. I liked him too much to stand in the way of his happiness.

"They're watching us," he said. It was true. We were surrounded, placed on a stage for an audience of onlookers.

A stage, or a cage? Even if our relationship hadn't been fake, would it have survived the scrutiny of Evermore High? The scrutiny of Click? High school relationships were fragile things, I decided, and they broke under the briefest of pressures. They were more fragile than a glass Christmas ornament. All it took was someone to brush against a branch, and the ornament would fall and shatter.

"I guess we need to give them something to watch," I said.

"Yeah…"

Chase took a deep breath. "So, this is it?"

His voice was loud. I'd heard him use it before — never to me, never to anyone in everyday life. It was the voice he used to call commands when he was playing football; the voice designed to carry over a field and above a crowd of cheering fans. A voice that would be caught by every camera within shouting distance.

Up close, it was over-powering.

My cheeks grew hot and my vision blurred. I rubbed the heel of my hand into my eyes. Then I mustered my strongest glare and shouted back. "This is what you wanted, isn't it? It's why you keep pushing me away. It's all for her."

There was a flash of confusion on Chase's face, but the cameras were on us, so he shook it off quickly. What was he confused about? It was the truth — this had all been to get Savannah back.

Chase's face contorted as he spoke again. "I did everything I could. Everything. But it wasn't enough. Well, you know what, Abigail Murrow? You're not perfect. You're just a girl."

And there it was, my greatest fear out in the open. I wasn't perfect. The same thing my mom had said to my dad before leaving. Chase's words opened an old scar. My spirit drained, and I lost any fight I had. In Chase's letter to Savannah, he had called her perfect. Something I would never be, no matter how hard I tried.

Tears welled in my eyes, and I blinked them furiously away before delivering my parting shot.

"We're done. At least someone got what they wanted." I pushed past Chase and stormed out of the quad.

CHASE

*M*y head spun.

I'd arrived in the quad to stop the breakup, to talk to Abby, but it all got out of control so fast, a car hitting black ice. The cameras came out, and we performed the perfect high school break up, complete with fake tears and a dramatic exit. I tried to make sense of it all, but it was like grasping for fog. No matter how hard I tried, answers slipped through my fingers.

What did she mean, "At least someone got what they wanted?" — by the look on her face, nobody had gotten what they wanted. I thought this was what she had decided. It was her decision to break up. So why did she look exactly like I felt?

Broken.

And what was I supposed to do now?

ABBY

*B*efore I'd even had time to return to my locker, Click exploded. The video of our breakup was everywhere. There were multiple fresh angles, infuriating captions, and worst of all, a trending hashtag: #Abbyaintperfect.

Way to rub that one in my face again. It was every nightmare I'd ever had come true. I sent a text to Izzy, told her I was turning off my phone, then drove home and cried myself to sleep in an empty house.

I felt cold and empty, and to make matters worse, I was harboring the searing realization that the only person I wanted to help make it better, was the one person I couldn't have: Chase. The memory of him telling me I wasn't perfect, eyes cold and mouth twisted, was burned indelibly on my frontal lobe. It was all I saw every time I closed my eyes.

It was meant to be a fake break up. Acting, staging a scene. So why did it feel so real? So raw? Tears welled up in my eyes every time I thought about it.

Keeping my new penchant for faking things going, I

pretended to have a stomach bug so I could miss the next two days of school. No way was I facing the music yet.

Instead, I wallowed in sad loneliness. Dad went to work after I insisted I was fine to stay home alone and Katie went to school. When they were both safely out of the way, I curled up on the couch, pajamas on, pint of ice cream in hand.

I was still all about the clichés.

I masochistically watched romantic comedy after romantic comedy. I resisted the urge to hurl things at the TV when they ended happily ever-after. Every. Single. Time.

I mean… come on. That wasn't real life. In real life, the all-star quarterback doesn't fall in love with the plain, socially awkward girl. He falls in love with the beautiful, redheaded, popular dancer or the cheerleading social media queen.

The perfect girls, perfectly matched for the perfect guy.

Tears stung my eyes every time I thought about how stupid I'd been to let myself develop genuine feelings for Chase freaking Jones. Our time together had been magical. During our fake relationship, I felt more like myself than I ever had. I confidently wore clothes that made me feel good rather than my uptight uniform. I socialized instead of holing up in my room and working. I was happy.

Chase let me discover who I really was, who I enjoyed being. It was my fault for blurring the lines between facade and reality. It had just been so easy to slip behind that curtain, to ignore my real life on the other side. I was the actress who lived the role of a lifetime and now had to go back to being a normal person.

Two days into my wallowing, I still wasn't brave enough to turn on my phone. Click was too much to take right now. And then there was the other issue: what if Chase texted me? Or worse, what if he hadn't?

The reality of that would be too much to bear. He would be too busy with Savannah to text. We weren't even real friends. Our social worlds never collided. It had been a pact of convenience, and that pact was now over.

To add to my list of current life grievances, the social feature was due soon — Nicholas had given me a deadline of next week, as he thought it would be a great lead-in for the upcoming Christmas Crush.

Nicholas had sent me an email yesterday, excited about the upcoming feature. It turned out EVERYONE wanted to know what I had to say about the social lives of Evermore High. This would be the first time people actually read the paper. But they weren't doing it because my investigative journalism skills fascinated them. They wanted the dirt, the cheap gossip. They wanted me to take subtle shots at Chase. Worse — they'd be looking for ways to misconstrue anything I wrote so it looked like I attacked Chase.

Over the weekend, I opened and closed my laptop a thousand times, never writing more than two words. I no longer cared about impressing Nicholas, or Mr. Adebayo, or anyone. When I wasn't staring at a blank page, I was curled up in my bed or eating food I couldn't taste. I still didn't turn my phone on. Maybe I would never turn it on again.

All I wanted to do was text Chase. I could play it cool and joke about our fake breakup, then add that I hoped he could be happy with Savannah, and that I hoped we could catch the saboteur soon. But I couldn't muster the courage.

I missed him. Badly. But I feared that if I turned on my phone, I'd have no messages from Chase, and way too many from Click.

The ones that yelled at me wouldn't bother me — what could words do when your heart was broken? — but if there were any pictures of Chase with Savannah together, news about them making up and starting over... I wouldn't be able to take it.

Better to stay ignorant and pretend Chase was as miserable as I was.

43

CHASE

I stood on the sidelines, my helmet in my hand, and watched the game clock tick down.

Five.

Four.

Three.

Two.

One.

Game over.

The River Valley High Warriors fans burst into cheers. Their school fight song played. Players leaped around the field and dog-piled on their quarterback. They were going to the state championship, and we weren't. We'd been up by a touchdown at the end of the first half, but then the running back who had replaced Dylan missed a block. As a result, I took a blindside hit and was knocked out for a few seconds.

The concussion spotter pulled me from the game as the world swirled in circles around me. After a flicker of his flashlight in both of my eyes, I was benched for the rest of the game, relegated to look on hopelessly at the mess that unfolded.

With Dylan, Adam and now me out of the game, it meant our offense was playing with a backup quarterback, a backup running back, and second-string receivers. Peter Landry, our backup QB, was good, but not good enough out there alone against the Warriors vaunted defense. We couldn't move the ball.

And so, we lost.

The locker room was quiet. A few of the seniors had tears in their eyes. The season was over, and for most of them, this would be the last time they played football. Coach Clarence made a speech about how proud he was of all of us, how proud he was that we fought so hard, but I didn't hear it. I'm not sure anyone did.

After you're eliminated from the playoffs, you have nightmares about it. You think about the plays you left on the field. The mistakes you made. Everything is magnified. If you could've just done this one thing differently, maybe it would've turned the tide. If you'd thrown that pass harder, if you'd made that block, if you hadn't fumbled…

I showered slowly, holding my throbbing head in my hands as the scalding water hit my aching back. I felt like I was carrying the weight of the world on my shoulders.

Payton, the reporter from the Pinnacle, was waiting for me outside the locker room. This wasn't surprising. She interviewed me after every game. Payton said that since I was the star quarterback, I was the person everyone wanted to hear from. I disagreed. Anyway, the way this week had gone — first the break up with Abby, then getting eliminated — the last thing I wanted to do was another interview.

Her expression softened when she saw me. "Tough game."

"Yeah," I mumbled. "Look, I know you need your story, but I hope you don't have too many questions, I'm not sure I'm up for it."

I tapped my head, trying to inject some humor into the situation.

"I'll walk with you to your car." Payton said. It was a statement, not a question. What was with these persistent school reporters?

The thought immediately made me think of Abby, which made my head throb even harder. I had scoured the bleachers for her after running onto the field earlier. The Friday night lights were blinding, but they didn't hide the truth: she wasn't there. She'd never come to a football game before we dated, so why would she come now that we were broken up?

The staged break up had been intense. The look she had on her face as we pretended to argue still haunted me. The argument almost felt... real. I texted her afterwards to check she was ok.

Chase: Wow, that was a good performance. You didn't tell me you were such a good actress! I tried my best, but it was tough... are you ok? So, what do we do next? What do you think the saboteurs next move will be?

Chase: Abby? Is everything ok?

Chase: Abby, please talk to me? Did something happen?

Chase: Abby, are you mad at me? Please talk to me?

Chase: ???

I'd eventually given up, hurt that she was ignoring me. She didn't need me anymore, so clearly she didn't even want to be friends now that she was done with her use for me.

"Chase? I said I'll walk you to your car." Payton's voice catapulted me back to reality.

"Oh sorry, uh, no... Jordyn's driving me," I told her. "Protocol says you can't drive yourself if you've been pulled out of the game with an injury. Especially a concussion."

"Is that why you left the game?"

The question irritated me. Of course it was why I left the

game. True, we'd been struggling even when I was in the game, but at least we'd moved the ball between the twenties. I blinked away my frustration and tried to sound nice as I answered.

"Yeah. Tough to win when you lose guys like Dylan and Adam to injury. But we can't make excuses. I thought the guys replacing them played well. Hand it to the Warriors — they're a talented team. Excellent defense. They'll be tough to beat."

It was a standard 'losing quarterback gives interview' response. You never threw a teammate under the bus. But the truth was, Dylan and Adam would have made a major difference. Dylan rarely missed a block and would have stopped the hit that took me out of the game. Adam could have run circles around the Warriors' secondary. If they were healthy, I believed we would have won. But I couldn't say that.

We reached the parking lot.

"That's all I need," Payton said. "Thanks."

I smiled dumbly, not bothering to respond. I was exhausted.

I waited for her to leave, but she kept walking beside me.

"I heard about you and Abby."

Ugh, great. Everyone had heard about us, thanks to stupid Click. I had to watch my break up on repeat. Sometimes in slow motion. Sometimes with auto-tune. But worse, I had to see Abby's expression repeatedly on screen: numb, then hurt.

I wished she would talk to me.

"I guess you aren't going to the Christmas Crush with her, hey?" Payton asked.

"Guess not." Was she trying to rub salt into the wound or what? Just leave me alone.

I tried to keep walking, to get away from her, before her

next question hit me in the back: "Do you want to go with me?"

Her request caught me by complete surprise. Our relationship — if you could call it that — was strictly professional. She reported on sports, I gave interviews. I could count on one-hand the amount of times we'd talked outside of official interviews, usually chatting in passing at parties.

"I'm not—" I began.

She cut me off. "Oh no, I mean… Not like that. Just as friends. I can help you keep your mind off things. No one should be alone at the Christmas Crush." She placed her hand on my shoulder. It was a strange gesture that felt weirdly invasive. I had an overwhelming urge to pick up her hand and remove it from me. But that would have been a bit too rude — she was just trying to help.

"Thanks," I said. "But I'll pass."

"Oh." Was there actual hurt in her voice?

"It's not you," I said quickly, never wanting to disappoint anyone as usual. "I just… I don't think I'm going with anyone to the Christmas Crush this year."

"Oh." Her tone was brighter. "Well, if you change your mind…"

"Okay." I just wanted the conversation to end.

She skipped away. Finally.

I turned around to find Jordyn, wanting more than anything to go home. I guess there was a first time for everything.

Jordyn sat in the driver's seat of her car waiting for me, a suspicious expression on her face.

44

ABBY

*M*y first day back at Evermore was like being the star of my own reality show. Everywhere I went, someone was trying to take a photo, or a video, while I kept my gaze focused on the linoleum tile of the hallway floor. Last thing I wanted to do was run into Madison. Or Savannah. Or Jordyn. Or Dylan. Or Chase.

Especially not Chase.

Somehow, in the matter of a couple of months I had gone from invisible to gossip mill sensation, with a complete laundry list of people I needed to try my best to avoid. On my way to the Pinnacle's office, a girl even slipped in close behind me and Izzy and tried to record our conversation. Izzy put a quick stop to that. I still hadn't turned on my phone, but Izzy's wouldn't stop vibrating with updates from Click.

She gave me a hug outside the office door. "You're sure about this? You will get in heaps of trouble."

"It's the right thing to do," I said.

"They might kick you off the paper."

"They might." I couldn't imagine what my mom would

191

say if I lost my position on the school paper. What I was about to do would burn my dreams of going to NYU. But sometimes you needed to start a fire — if it was the right thing to do.

And this felt right.

The familiar aroma of coffee strong enough to do pushups surrounded me as I entered the office. The normally constant chatter dropped to nothing as everyone's eyes fell on me.

"Show's over," Nicholas said, standing. "Back to work, everyone. We've all been there. All done that. Everyone move along. And if I catch any of you even opening Click while you're in this office — you'll be removed from the paper. Abby, come with me?"

We went to the back office, and I sat at the desk across from him. He smiled at me kindly, and I smiled back, weakly. How could I have ever thought I liked Nicholas? Looking at him now, I realized that everything I had ever felt for the paper's lead editor paled in comparison for my feelings for Chase.

"Thanks," I said.

"How are you holding up?"

A few months ago, I would've given anything to have Nicholas ask me something personal. But now all I wanted to do was deflect the attention away from me. "I've been better."

"I bet." He leaned forward in his chair, concerned. "So, Abby. You said you needed to talk to me."

"I do."

It was time to do the hardest thing.

♥

Suspension.

The word drowned out everything. I'd done what was

right, and Nicholas had suspended me from the paper for the rest of the semester. He said that while he understood where I was coming from, he needed to set an example. He also said that he felt that I needed some time away from everything, and that he hoped he might reinstate me in January.

I'd have to cross my fingers.

The other journalists buried their noses in their work, making it all too obvious that they'd been trying to eavesdrop. Fortunately, both Nicholas and I spoke softly. I doubt they'd heard anything yet, and he would announce his decision to them shortly after I finished packing up my stuff.

Payton was sitting next to my bag, her life scattered across the table in front of her. She was editing pictures of the last football game. The one I hadn't been at. The one Evermore lost, knocking them out of the championship.

It hurt to think about. Had our break up made Chase play poorly? Did he lose his focus? Was I the cause of the biggest failure in his football career? Was I being way too egotistical to think I could even affect his gameplay at all?

I fought away the thoughts before tears welled.

Then, scattered among all the notes across Payton's desk, something caught my eye. A piece of paper with Chase's handwriting on it — unmistakably Chase's handwriting. Messy. Barely legible. Why would Payton have a letter from Chase?

I pretended to reach for a pencil across the table, dropping my elbow low enough to move the rest of the papers out of the way. I skimmed the note.

Ah.

It was just his fake news article, the one he used to invite me to the Christmas Crush. My heart hurt, looking at his scratchy handwriting. He tried so hard on that one. He must have had Payton help him turn it into newspaper format. It made sense — she's the only person he knew at the Pinnacle besides me.

I left without saying a word.

Izzy was waiting outside. "How'd it go?"

"Suspension. To be re-evaluated in January."

She squeezed my shoulder. "You did the right thing."

"Thanks." We left the Fine Arts building and stepped out into the late November chill. "How long do you think before Madison asks Chase to the Christmas Crush?"

"Don't think she will," Izzy said. "Apparently she's going with Jebidiah Moose."

"For real?!" So the rumor that Madison was dating a famous YouTube star was true. I had heard that months ago, but just assumed it was a decoy for her to get Chase back. In fact, I'd fully expected her to move in on Chase at the first available opportunity. But if she had, it would have been all over Click, and Izzy would have seen it. Why would she sabotage his relationships and then not make a move?

"I don't think Chase is going with anyone," Izzy said. "He looked so sad after you guys broke up that apparently the only person who even tried to make a move was Payton, but—"

"WHAT?" I yelped like a startled puppy.

Izzy looked surprised for a second before understanding dawned on her face. "This happens at Evermore when you don't look at Click. You lose out on the hot gossip. Apparently, Payton asked Chase if he wanted to go to the Christmas Crush with her right after they lost. Terrible time to ask because—"

"Shh…" My brain was in overload.

Payton.

Payton, who had specifically requested to be the journalist covering our football team for the year.

Payton, who had interviewed Chase after every football game.

Payton, who was at Peak's the morning the saboteur sent me the photo of Chase and "Savannah."

Payton, who was so good with Photoshop that she could manipulate a photo to make Jordyn look like Savannah.

Payton, who had access to a letter written by Chase, IN HIS OWN HANDWRITING — a letter she could manipulate into anything she wanted. Even a love letter.

It was Payton all along.

45

CHASE

*I*t was tough to avoid everyone when you were the starting quarterback after an enormous loss — and a public breakup. People were either trying to capture everything I did on Click or they were making choking motions behind my back. Never mind the fact that I hadn't played the whole second half. Evermore was never the place to let the truth impede a good story.

When anyone asked why I was so down, I told them I was upset that I had lost the big game. But the truth?

It hurt to lose the game.

It hurt more to lose Abby. I'd tried texting her, then texting Izzy when Abby didn't reply. Izzy was cold and told me that Abby was keeping her phone off for a bit. She wasn't used to being dumped while the spotlight was shining.

I held my tongue.

I wished I could keep my phone off. At one point, Savannah stopped me unexpectedly to see how I was doing. She touched my elbow for the briefest of moments — and someone captured the moment and blasted it all over Click:

"Chase and Savannah — Back Together!" Hashtag NewIt-Couple. I wanted to explain to Abby that it wasn't what it looked like, but she was a ghost.

The entire week leading up to the Christmas Crush, I kept my eyes peeled for her. But I never saw her.

♥

"HE WILL NOT SNAP out of it." Jordyn said. "He's been like this for the last two weeks. You'd think he actually liked this one." She raised her eyebrow, but I said nothing. I knew she was trying to get a rise out of me.

While Click, and therefore the rest of school, had moved on from my breakup with Abby — I owed the mysterious Trey Carter big time for taking the heat off me, he had been spotted at the police precinct for who knows what — Jordyn had pestered me non-stop.

What happened with Abby?

Why aren't you hanging out with Abby?

When will you tell me about Abby?

Admittedly, at this point I was refusing to tell her out of spite.

"Dude. Come on." Dylan stood beside Jordyn. They were both staring into my bedroom where I was lying on my bed in a suit. "It's the Christmas Crush. You have to come."

"Why?" I closed my eyes

"Because." Dylan faltered.

"Wonderful reason, champ." Jordyn put her hands on her hips and glared towards Dylan. He turned to look at her, slightly mesmerized — my sister was angry, her face red above her navy silk dress. She was terrifying.

"I didn't hear you coming up with a better idea," Dylan said.

"That's because you talked before I could think."

"Guess I'm too fast for you."

"Word of advice — it's not always a good thing for a guy to be fast," Jordyn snapped.

"If you both shut up, I'll come to the stupid dance," I said, raising my voice slightly. They sounded like an old married couple.

Dylan and Jordyn had been nice enough to abandon their own dates to take me. I was equal parts mortified and touched by this gesture, but neither of them seemed to mind too much.

"See!" Dylan said. "It worked."

Jordyn put her hands on her hips again — it was starting to be her signature maneuver. "Whatever."

I stood and dusted off my suit. So, I was doing it. I would go to the Christmas Crush. I must still be concussed.

"Is Abby going to be there?"

Jordyn gasped. "She who must not be named!"

"I just want to know if I'm just going to be used again," I said bitterly.

"You're so dramatic," Jordyn said — you guessed it, while rolling her eyes. "Name one time Abby used you."

"How about our entire relationship? She was just using me so she could get into all the cool events for the social feature."

Jordyn and Dylan both stared at me blankly.

I sighed. "The one she published this week in the lead up to the Christmas Crush?" I hadn't opened the Pinnacle's website or picked up a physical paper either, but I knew her article was due to be published last week and I didn't think I could stomach reading it.

"Oh give me a break," Jordyn said. "As if she would do that. Abby's nice. Anyway, I can prove you wrong, because

Abby didn't publish anything this week. In fact, she got suspended from the Pinnacle."

"What!? Why?"

"Ask her yourself." Jordyn plucked my phone from my hand. "In person. At the Christmas Crush."

46

CHASE

*T*he Christmas Crush.

Imagine every Christmas decoration you could find crammed into the grand room of the nicest hotel in town. In the center was a giant Christmas tree, perfectly decorated with colorful lights, giant ornaments, and a star at the top. The tree was probably three stories high and nearly touched the vaulted ceiling.

In one corner, there was a giant gingerbread house that you could walk through. Every student at Evermore was using it as a photo op — several of them pretending to bite the ceiling or the fake candy canes in the driveway.

Jordyn gagged, unimpressed. "Do they realize that they're all biting and licking the same place? Disgusting."

Dylan laughed. "Welcome to every day at Evermore High."

On the other side of the grand room was a line of tables, lit by rows of twinkling fairy lights, holding punch bowls that were sure to be spiked with liquor at some point tonight by a wayward student, and countless platters of Christmas cookies and cupcakes.

And in the middle of it all?

The dance floor, which circled around the Christmas tree. Every student at Evermore was here, decked out in their formal clothes. Evermore High took the Christmas Crush seriously, and the guys had all come in suits, the girls in prom dresses. Under the glittering, twinkling lights, a sea of students swayed to the slow music. A few of the teachers were chaperoning the proceedings, and they hovered on the edge of the dancefloor almost nervously, clutching paper cups of punch.

"Does anyone see her?" I asked.

Jordyn pointed. "There. Staring at the tree like she's a kid."

Jordyn's description was accurate.

There Abby was, standing and staring up at the beautiful Christmas tree, her face aglow in the reflection of the lights, looking just like a child whose imagination had been captured.

Somehow, I'd forgotten how breathtaking she was.

Abby wore a beautiful deep green formal dress and her dark hair tumbled long and loose down her back, save for a section that was woven into a beautiful braid crown along the side of her head. She looked like — excuse the cliché — a princess.

Her eyes glowed the same color as her dress. Emerald.

She stood next to the tree, her hands interlaced behind her back, the soft glow of the colored Christmas lights dancing along her face. I realized, sadly, that unless she had convinced her father to change his mind, this would be the only Christmas tree she'd get this year.

"Abby," I walked up and stood behind her, my heart thumping out of my chest.

She turned.

"I wanted to—"

She held up her hand, cutting me off. "Me first."

"It was Payton," Abby said, a sad smile on her face. "She was the person behind everything. She photoshopped pictures of you with another girl and sent them to Savannah."

WHAT? Payton? The reporter?

I tried to speak, but she held her hand up again.

"And, before you say anything, there's something I need to tell you. I have a confession," Abby said.

I stood still, rooted to the spot. A confession? About what?

"I don't like Nicholas. Honestly, after feeling the things I felt for you, I don't know if I ever did. Not really. And… I lied. I don't date outside the school. In fact, I don't date. Ever. At all. I never dated anyone before you. And I know all of this was fake, but it felt real to me. And you were the best boyfriend a girl could want. I just wanted you to know that." Abby fought back tears. "I knew I needed to make it right, so I explained everything about the saboteur to her."

Abby gestured sadly and out of nowhere a girl glided across the dance floor and stepped between Abby and I before I could speak.

Savannah? What was going on? What had Abby done?

Savannah took my hand. "It's true. I'm sorry, I should've said something to you after Abby told me, but you've been hard to reach."

My brain was melting, barely able to process the fact that Savannah was now standing in front of me. Payton had sabotaged my relationships? Abby had real feelings for me?

As soon as Abby and I broke up, Payton invited me to the Christmas Crush. She had done this so she could have a chance to be with me? Anger fought with a thousand other emotions as I tried to comprehend what was happening.

Savannah squeezed my hand. "It's okay. Abby explained everything to me. Why don't we start over?"

"I…"

I looked for Abby, but she was already gone.

47

ABBY

I hurried through the crowd, not even stopping to say hi to Jordyn and Dylan. The Christmas tree had been so beautiful. For the brief moment I was staring at it, I was at peace. Then Chase had arrived. I'd avoided him completely since the breakup. The only news I heard was through Izzy, who relayed that someone sent a Click blast of him with Savannah.

Even if the letter wasn't real, they both deserved to know who broke them up. It wasn't fair to either of them, what Payton had done. Maybe they could have a second chance.

A chance I would never have.

Izzy was waiting by the door. I'd told her everything a few days ago, the whole truth, and nothing but the truth. It was good to have everything off my chest, and I was thankful to have a forgiving best friend who was always there for me.

She immediately put her arm around me and guided me out of the hotel. Adam Zamos was standing near the exit. He tried to take a photo of me while I was leaving — probably for Click — but Hailey was next to him and ruthlessly slapped his phone out of his hand. The screen shattered as his phone skirted across the tile.

We were in Izzy's car when I broke down, my chest heaving with sobs. My heart had broken twice. Once when Chase and I ended our "fake" relationship. Then again when I gave him over to the perfect girl. But that's what he deserved. Perfect. And that's what I wasn't.

"You'll be okay," Izzy said. "Do you want to go home?"

I shook my head. "Can I stay with you?"

"Always."

I'd fulfilled my end of the bargain to Chase.

48

CHASE

"*I*'m sorry," I said. "I can't."

Savannah let go of my hand. "It's her... isn't it?"

"I'm sorry, Savannah. I'm sorry Payton hurt you and made you think I had hurt you." I floundered, not sure exactly what to say.

Savannah smiled warmly. "Chase, I saw your face a moment ago. I saw the way you looked at her. You love her, don't you?"

Shock coursed through me at Savannah's words. You love her, don't you...

That was it.

I loved her.

I was in love with Abby.

Savannah adjusted my jacket. "Hey, go get her. You guys are great together."

"Thank you, Savannah." I flung my arms around her in a quick, friendly hug, and she smiled again. One day, she would find someone amazing.

I had to go get Abby.

I crossed the dance floor, swerving in and out of

swaying couples. I was desperately trying to think of my next move. How could I win Abby back? Where had she gone? I stopped suddenly as someone stepped in front of me, blocking my path. Payton Clarence stood in front of me. Oh great.

"Chase, can I—"

My glare silenced her. "No, Payton, you can't. Whatever it is. You've done enough."

I walked away. Payton Clarence wasn't worth a second thought.

I had something way more important to do.

I tried to call, but her phone was still off. I'd seen her for only a heartbeat, but it was the first time I'd felt alive since our break up.

Where was she? Did she run off to the bathroom? Somewhere else?

"Have you seen her?" I shouted at Jordyn, barging over to interrupt her slow dance with Peter Landry.

She dropped Peter's hands immediately, turned away from him, and motioned for me to come closer. "She left with Izzy."

"Going where?" I asked impatiently. Poor Peter was looking at Jordyn's back dejectedly.

"I don't know… I didn't even get to speak to her. She was in too much of a hurry. She looked pretty upset, though." Jordyn punched my shoulder. "Did you do something moronic again?"

"Probably," I admitted. "I need to find her."

"Hey, what happened with Abby?" Dylan walked up, hand in hand with a cute girl I recognized from the cheerleading team, Lauren something-or-other.

"I'm gonna go get her."

"Dude, what about the after party?" Dylan asked.

"This is more important. I need to find her." I stopped,

realizing I had driven Dylan and Jordyn here. I looked at my sister. "Can you find a way home?"

"I'll protect your sister, dude," Dylan said, puffing out his chest.

"Great, we'll be dead by dawn," Jordyn said sarcastically. "Go on. Save the day. Win the touchdown. Whatever it is you do."

I hustled out of the Christmas Crush. Hailey and Adam were arguing about something by the door, but then again, they always seemed to be arguing recently.

I hopped in my Jeep and drove straight to Abby's house.

I rang the doorbell, shifting my weight from foot to foot, impatient.

Please be home.

Please be home.

The door opened.

Her dad.

"Chase? Shouldn't you be at the Christmas Crush?"

"Is Abby here? I really need to talk to her."

"She's staying at Izzy's." His expression was grim. "And are you sure she wants to talk to you? I heard about what happened, you know." He folded his arms.

I forced myself to keep eye contact. I saw mistrust in his eyes. "I'm sorry, sir. I'm trying to make it right."

A flash of inspiration hit.

"I have an idea," I said.

49

ABBY

I spent the night of the Christmas Crush watching slasher movies at Izzy's house, reveling in the gore splattering on the screen, a welcome change of pace from my thoughts. Izzy tried to distract me, but my mind was stuck on Chase.

Did I make the right decision? Should I have told him about how I truly felt instead of throwing Savannah at him?

No, that wouldn't be fair. It was Savannah he wanted.

So what now? Were we friends again? Could I be friends with him? And what was he doing at the Christmas Crush? With Savannah?

What were they doing together?

The last question filled me with both heartbreak and jealousy, but it was the question I kept coming back to. What were they doing together? Were they a couple now?

Had they kissed?

I could see it — Chase, handsome in his suit like the Chase of my black-and-white movie dreams, kissing the beautiful fairytale princess for a happy ending. My fingers curled, my nails digging into my palm. Why did doing the right thing feel so wrong?

Eventually, even with the thoughts racing around my head, I fell asleep to the sound of screaming and stabbing on the screen in front of me.

I woke the next morning with a pounding head, still in my stupid prom dress. I hadn't bothered to change, though Iz had offered me a pair of pajamas.

Izzy drove me home. I thanked my friend over and over for putting up with my misery. I needed to get home as soon as I could. I wanted to sit down and cry, but I didn't want to do it in front of Izzy. Again.

We pulled up to my house and my breath caught in my throat.

Chase's Jeep was outside.

Chase's Jeep was outside MY HOUSE.

I turned to look at Izzy, her eyes were huge and round. "Uh, Abs? Chase Jones is in your house."

"Why? Why? WHY would he be here?" Was he here to thank me for setting him up with Savannah or something?

Izzy gave me a huge hug. "Relax. You're beautiful and special and wonderful, and if Chase Jones doesn't see that, it's his loss."

The tears were already starting. What was I going to find when I went inside? Was this goodbye?

I approached my house slowly, almost like it was a deer that might prance away if I moved too fast. My thoughts got progressively more upsetting as I walked towards my front door.

Why was Chase Jones at my house the morning after the Christmas Crush?

Why wasn't he with Savannah?

Was he with Savannah? Were they here together, as a couple?

Should I check Click before going inside?

No, I didn't have time. There were probably a thousand messages waiting for me on Click — and nine hundred and ninety-nine of them would be nasty.

I opened the door, my heart in my throat. "Hello?"

Dad was in the kitchen with Katie, making breakfast. They looked totally normal, like nothing was happening. Katie was sitting on a barstool, sipping orange juice. Extra pulp.

"Morning, Abby," Dad smiled.

What the…?

I looked back outside the window to confirm what I had thought I'd seen. Yes, Chase's Jeep was still out there. He was here… somewhere.

"Is—"

"In your room," Dad said.

Chase Jones was in my bedroom? What? Why? Had I cleaned? Was it a mess? WHY WAS HE IN MY BEDROOM? Emotions went to war in my chest. Hope threw punches at fear. Anxiety battled with excitement.

I climbed the stairs one by one, my dress dragging on the ground as my bare feet padded forward — I had long abandoned my heels from the night before.

My bedroom door was open.

There was a soft glow emanating from the doorway.

Almost like…

Like…

I stood in the door.

Chase Jones was standing in the middle of my room. Chase Jones, still in his suit from the night before. His dark hair flopping over his navy eyes. Navy eyes that were gazing at me and made me want to melt into a puddle on the spot.

The pounding in my heart grew deafening.

Behind Chase, in the corner of my bedroom, was a

Christmas tree, lit up in a million different colors of twinkling Christmas lights. The glow of the colored lights reached across the ceiling, filling every nook and cranny of the room. Snowflakes and candy canes and garlands and tinsel hung from each branch.

My jaw dropped. "How…"

"I talked to your dad," Chase said. "I told him how much it meant to you. How much you wanted a Christmas tree. I begged him to let me put one up. He helped, but it took most of the night."

I was speechless.

Chase's smile was restrained. "Abby, I need you to answer something."

How could I refuse?

"Did you get suspended from the Pinnacle because you didn't publish the social feature?"

"Yes." My voice was soft.

"I know how much that meant to you. That was the whole point of our… thing. Why didn't you publish it?"

The question that I'd avoided for the last two weeks.

The answer I wouldn't tell my dad.

I wouldn't tell Katie.

I wouldn't even tell Izzy.

Could I tell Chase?

I took a deep breath. The world was spinning. Was I actually about to do this? Was I actually about to SAY this?

"I didn't publish the social feature…"

For someone who prided themselves on being good with words, I was sure struggling with them.

I cleared my throat, wet my lips, and tried again. "The social feature was a collection of all of my memories of you. Of us. Those memories weren't for everyone. I wanted to keep that part of you for me."

It happened like something out of a black and white movie.

Chase was the leading man, still wearing his suit, crossing the room.

I stepped to meet him, stepped on my tiptoes, my heart hammering.

His hand, brushing the hair from my eyes, warm against my cheek, then the back of my neck as he gently pulled me towards him.

I tilted my chin.

Closed my eyes.

Our lips met with the softness of a snowflake on a river. He pulled my body tight to his, and I felt his strength and warmth through the thin fabric of his shirt. I threw my arms around his broad shoulders and pulled him as close as I could. There were a thousand words I could use to describe my first kiss, but I only needed one:

Electric.

50

ABBY

*B*y Christmas morning, we had moved the huge Christmas tree into the living room.

In the buildup to Christmas day, Katie, Dad, Chase, and I decorated the entire house with the most obnoxiously messy decorations we could find. We looped garlands around stair rails, hung plastic Dollar Store snowflakes from mirrors, draped tinsel on the mantel, and every table had its own snow globe. We even strung Christmas lights along the fence in the backyard.

It was a tacky, beautiful, perfect winter wonderland. And my heart was warm.

On Christmas Day, Chase and Jordyn arrived shortly after breakfast. Apparently, their parents were fighting again, and they were looking for a reason to get out of their house.

We drank hot apple cider and laughed at my Dad's stupid Christmas jokes and played games, and when it came time to tear into presents, Chase slid a little box in my direction.

"Here," he said.

He bought me a gift?

As if reading my mind, Chase laughed. "What, Abby, can't your boyfriend buy you a Christmas gift?"

Boyfriend.

There it was, that magic, wonderful word that I couldn't get enough of hearing. And this time, it was real. Real real real. Chase was all mine.

The gift was a necklace: an intricate snowflake on a delicate silver chain.

"It's beautiful."

"All snowflakes are unique, just like you." Chase smiled. "Just a little reminder that you are amazing, just the way you are. You don't need to pretend to be anything else to anybody. Ever."

It was perfect. And Chase was right.

Over the past few months I had learned so much. I didn't need to be perfect, or prove myself to everyone. The only person who I needed to be was me. Chase had helped show me that. Gone were my uncomfortable office clothes that I wore just for people to take me seriously. I enjoyed dressing more casually and feeling cute in what I wore when Chase and I were faking it. So much so that Izzy, Katie and I had gone on a huge shopping trip to pick out clothes I liked. Clothes that made me feel good exactly the way I was. No more playing a part.

Also gone was my incessant need to achieve, replaced by a desire to do things I actually liked. Payton had quit the Pinnacle last week, too embarrassed to cover sports anymore after what she had done to the quarterback.

I still wanted to go to NYU, but I started researching other journalism programs as options for me. I wanted to make sure I picked the course that worked for my hopes and dreams — and not my mother's.

I spoke to Nicholas about trying my hand at sports journalism after my suspension was lifted. It was a great way to try my hand at a new skill I enjoyed — gossip free! I loved going to football games. And I definitely loved a certain star quarterback.

After we opened gifts, Jordyn, Chase, and I headed to the Riverwalk where we met up with Dylan and Izzy.

We walked along the beautifully lit pathways, shivering in the cold as we went. Swirls of snow drifted lazily across the pathway.

Chase and I lagged behind.

The Monday after our first kiss, I arrived at Evermore wearing Chase's football jacket. There was no need to make a big production of it. Abigail Murrow and Chase Jones were officially together.

It didn't take long for someone to capture us on video, kissing in the parking lot. The kiss got so much attention on Click that the app went offline for fifteen minutes, but neither of us cared — we'd both deleted it. We were in this relationship together, and we would not let something like a stupid app get in our way.

We were in this together.

As I shivered my way along the Riverwalk, Chase put his arm around me and gently kissed the top of my head. "So, what do you think?"

"What do I think about what?"

"This." He slipped a piece of paper into my hand.

51

CHASE

I watched Abby unfold the piece of paper.

She laughed.

It was the checklist we'd created together, the pact outlining the rules for our "Strictly Business" fake relationship. It felt like forever ago, like something from another lifetime. And as for our relationship? It was real now. And, if I was being honest, it was real then, too.

She was all mine.

We agreed to tell no one. Why complicate things? That was one thing I loved about Abby — and there were a million of them. Even when things were complicated, she made them feel simple. Like there was always a right answer.

We walked over to a fire pit where a handful of kids were roasting marshmallows.

Abby crumpled the checklist and tossed it in the fire. "That's what I think of that agreement!"

Our eyes met.

"I love you, Abigail Murrow."

She smiled. "I love you too, Chase Jones."

I pulled her close and kissed her.

She'd never admit it, but she was perfect.

Thank you so much for reading!

If you enjoyed this book, please leave me a review. As a new author, reviews mean everything to me. I appreciate each and every one of them.